Flourish:
Award Winning Original
Australian Short Stories

Other books from Morrison Mentoring:

Summer

Glint

Flourish:
Award Winning Original Australian Short Stories

Edited by Catie Morrison

Morrison Mentoring

2015

First Printing: 2015

ISBN 978-0-9941631-2-7

Morrison Mentoring
Mount Waverley
Victoria, Australia, 3149

www.morrisonmentoring.com.au

Ordering Information:
Special discounts are available on quantity purchases by corporations, associations, educators, and others. For details, contact the publisher.

Trade bookstores and wholesalers: Please contact Morrison Mentoring. Tel: +61 4 1236 0528 email catie@morrisonmentoring.com.au

Dedication

To the inspiring authors whose works are contained herein, and to all who seek "human flourishing" via the written word.

Contents

Preface

Morrison Mentoring is pleased to present this anthology of award-winning fiction, from among entries to the 2015 Short Story Writing Competition. The theme of the competition was "Flourish", and authors were invited to respond to this theme, however tangentially. Winning and highly commended entries are included in this volume.

The winning entries were:

Open to all Australian Residents:
"Iggy Poop" by Casey Millikin

Secondary School:
"Nature Reclaims" by Brynnie Rafe

Speculative Fiction:
"Spirit of the Earth" by Pamela Jeffs

The Speculative Fiction category was new this year, and was well represented among entries, showcasing Australia's exciting SF community.

I trust you'll enjoy reading these original pieces by talented Australian authors. For information about forthcoming short story writing competitions, please visit the Morrison Mentoring website at www.morrisonmentoring.com.au.

Catie Morrison

"Calculating Coffees", by Alicia Bruzzone

Jared was desperate. Three weeks he'd been lugging this coffee van around to the train station every morning, and for three weeks every morning he'd had as many customers as he could count on his hands. One day he'd had twelve, and it had been occasion to celebrate; he'd made enough money to cover the cost of milk. That only left the rental fee of the cumbersome truck in deficit. There was a point where Optimism died and took its friends Hope and Future down with it.

He'd run his numbers, more times than he cared to admit, but it wasn't like he was busy serving customers. It didn't make sense. He was in the car park of one of the busiest train stations on the network, the morning city commuters pouring past him as he attempted to hold his cheery smile in place. It was getting harder and harder to slap there every morning, and with each passing set of legs that neglected to stop. The coffee was good, he'd tried it, but Jared had to convince everyone else of that fact. Or else he'd loose everything. It was rush hour, the place swarmed with desperate office workers and business women in tailored suits and business men in ties that would pay his rent for the fortnight. Okay, maybe not the fortnight, but things were looking bleak. Everyone loved coffee, and city workers needed the morning pick me up more than anyone. Jared was stumped. Why was it nothing he ever did worked, no matter how hard he worked, no matter how much planning and research went in beforehand? So much for his grand plan. He was barely surviving no way he'd make it to thriving, let alone flourishing.

A woman in a brown coat looked up from the pavement and caught sight of the van. Jared's heart stupidly beat faster, anticipation mounting as she glanced at her watch, and then kept walking. He sunk into the carpeted square behind the tailgate that constituted a seat, the rest of the space occupied by equipment and supplies. This wasn't going to work. He was going to be penniless and homeless and have his kids taken off him because no one wanted coffee. How could no one want to buy coffee?

Jared was tired. Tired of never being able to do anything right, no matter how hard he tried. Tired of struggling every day to no avail. Tired of every barb his ex-wife had ever used in discontentment proving true. He was no good, and he was never going to amount to anything. He couldn't sell coffee for Pete's sake.

A metallic wrap on the side panel brought him out of his stupor. Brown coat was back, giving him a wane smile. Irresponsibly, his heart picked up in rhythm again, a flurry of blood coursing with new speed to his extremities. Jared painted on his helpful smile and jumped to his feet. "What can I get you?"

It seemed a simple question in his mind, but the lady in the brown coat squinted at the board for several moments, and Jared's anxiety to make a sale spiked, funneling adrenaline through his cramping limbs. Great, now his hands were going to shake as he tried to heat the milk.

"Do you have hot chocolate?" the woman asked hopefully, eyebrows high over brown shaded eyelids.

Jared's stomach sank to his ankles. He had Arabica, Columbian, Brazilian, and Timor varieties; and five different types of milk; but no powdered chocolate. He was running a coffee van; he sold coffee. Hell, he could make an affogato if the need arose, just not a stinking hot chocolate. Of course he wouldn't think of that. Typical Jared.

"It's okay, just surprise me," the woman replied, obviously judging his answer from his contorted face. She was already rummaging in her handbag for coins to pay.

Coins. Jared's lifeline was being dolled out in twenty cent pieces. As she lined them up along the back Jared set to work, making the most impressive cappuccino he could muster. Maybe she'd tip him an extra forty cents.

Living the dream.

He pulled out his customer face before he turned, steaming coffee in hand. Happy coffee man living off nothing and falling backwards with phenomenal speeds.

She took the cup with a smile that looked more genuine than his, he was sure, and glanced down at the army of coins she'd deposited on the counter. All the coins were in piles of five, dollar amounts that represented a lot more than the cost of a coffee. "For tomorrow," she said, reading Jared's confusion. "I'll want a hot chocolate. That should cover your investment in a bag of cocoa. The secret is to add as much sugar as chocolate powder." She smiled a little wider, crinkles playing at the corners of her eyes and Jared stared like a floundering idiot. He wasn't sure he was going to be around long enough for her to drink through an entire bag of hot chocolate provisions. He had one week before he hit completely destitute.

The woman glanced nervously at her watch again, followed by an unconscious flick of her head to the train lines. Right, she had somewhere to be. "How's the coffee?" Jared asked, maybe a little too forcefully. He needed to know it didn't suck, that yes, people enjoyed his caffeinated beverages. That there was one thing he did right in this life, besides stick by his boys. He understood why their mother had abandoned them, but he would never do the same. All he needed was for people to like his stinking coffee.

The woman looked at her feet, old scuffed loafers that needed replacing six months back. "I don't actually drink coffee," she said a little breathlessly, a huff contained by a loud swallow in her throat. "I was going to give it to the guy in the ticket booth," she admitted guiltily. "You're parked on the wrong side of the track."

Pity coffee. Jared's fake smile must be holding out worse than he'd envisioned. "I don't suppose you have fifty friends also willing to place false orders?" he suggested, annoyed at how his life was panning out. Wrong side of the tracks indeed. It didn't matter how much of himself he'd poured into her cup, she wasn't going to taste it.

The woman laughed and brushed down the lapels of her coat. "I don't think the station hand would appreciate quite that many discarded coffees."

Jared frowned. Did nobody drink coffee anymore? It would account for his appalling sales. Maybe it had been declared carcinogenic or something in the last month and he hadn't noticed. Or he just sucked, as nothing he did was ever good enough, everything he touched turned to mushy piles of fermenting excrement.

"You're on the wrong side of the tracks," the woman repeated, her arm sweeping over the view of the platform.

Jared didn't follow. He was on the southbound side, where the largest amount of foot traffic was. This line fed straight into the city where most of the populace was employed.

Brown coat shook her head. "Most commuters don't want to be awake. They set an alarm on their phone and sleep until their stop. Hard to catch up on extra rest when you've just downed a coffee. And you would have to scull scalding coffee. The trains come every four minutes, and they don't allow food or drink on the carriages. If you want a morning coffee, you grab it in the city and sip on your way to work so you look perky when you get there." She pointed to the other side of the train station, the northbound platform that had people milling about. "That train runs every twenty minutes, which means those people have time to drink coffee when they show up early. You're on the wrong side of the tracks. Hightail it over there mornings and evenings, and I think you'll be okay". She gave him another friendly grin then hurried up the ramp to the platform as Jared puzzled it over.

Jared had discounted the north bound folks, assuming if they wanted coffee badly enough they'd walk up the set of steps, over the train lines, and down to this side. Maybe that was an oversight.

No one wanted to walk an extra four flights of stairs in the morning climbing over and back. Figuring he had nothing to loose, he collected the jingling piles of money and secured his equipment, closed the hatch on the boot, and wound himself onto the opposite platform. He opened up shop, and promptly sold twenty cups of coffee, to people who were actually drinking it. Not just drinking, but appearing to enjoy the experience. His insides perked at the possibility that they liked something he created. His ex was wrong; he wasn't useless at everything. Tomorrow he'd even have hot chocolates.

Jared was done living his life on the wrong side of the tracks. Next step thrive, then he'd flourish.

"Cooking with Concern", by Alicia Bruzzone

My fingers instinctively reached for my neck, playing on the two small puncture wounds I'd received on our last meeting. No way was I ever stepping into the hall to pay for my late night pizza delivery ever again. Thankfully there was still a door between us, and this time I only had the misfortune to view him through the peephole. "GO. AWAY."

Vampires. Who knew it wasn't just gothic teen folklore. Thankfully they got the glamouring part wrong, or the beguiling look I was getting through my peephole might be doing more damage. Though it was hard to look anything other than seedy when you had a ginger moustache beginning to form on your upper lip.

"Bianca, I truly am concerned." Reginald held a jar of multivitamins to the small circle of glass, his strawberry blond locks framed behind it. "I've got iron supplements too. May I come in?"

I swung open the door in a blind stupor of rage. "What, so you can insult me again?"

"You're smelling better already," he commented, disregarding my mood to casually step into my apartment. Reginald looked out of place in his designer suit jacket and snug fitting Levi jeans. He had a black t-shirt underneath, and with the charcoal jacket and faded blue denim he was really accentuating the pale highlights in his hair.

I was in yoga pants and a tank top I hadn't washed in a while, but the walls looked cleaner by contrast if I stayed a little grungy.

Reginald flicked his pointer finger towards the door, and it creaked before closing with a soft click. "Now, I've only got all night, did you start on the organic juicing regiment I suggested?"

I huffed and folded my arms over my chest, sulking that he had the nerve to show his face here after last time. He seemed to pick up my mood.

"Bianca, darling," Reginald drawled, a slight southern accent sticking to his tongue. His cold fingers played a shivering caress down my upper arm; a predator playing with his meal. "We've been through this. It really is not healthy. You already skipped the doctor's check up I made you. You can barely survive as you are; a young woman such as yourself should be flourishing."

I hated the way he sounded so concerned for me, like I was suffering from a terminal illness and he was trying to make me comfortable for death. I took his vitamins and threw them at the far wall. "There is nothing wrong with me!"

He tutted and looked down his nose at me, eyebrows rising into a cocky arch.

It wasn't my fault he hadn't liked my blood, and it wasn't as if I'd given him permission.

"Don't go blaming the garlic bread again, if you'd let me get the bloodwork done like I'd wanted I wouldn't have to treat you with such clumsy methodology." Reginald sounded like a headmaster scolding an unruly student.

"GO. AWAY." I repeated, knowing it would be to no avail. Reginald was a stubborn old undead bloodsucker.

He ignored me and folded into the couch, one leg elegantly crossing over the other. "This is a serious problem. I've never tasted anyone so foul who wasn't already dead."

There was a visual I didn't need. Reginald examined my television remote as if he'd never seen one. Maybe he just wasn't used to them being coated with sweet and sour sauce.

Reginald fixed his attention back to me when I ignored him. "Don't be like that, Bianca. You did get the gift I sent you?"

I threw my hands up in the air in exasperation. "You got me a cook book. Entitled: How to Taste Nice." He didn't seem to grasp the reason for my lack of gratitude. "I don't want to taste good. I don't want to be your meal partner, and I don't want you, or any other vampire in my life."

"They say it's the thought that counts," he replied, eyes crossing as he managed to look offended by my comments.

"Then think about cleaning the dried blood spurts off my rug!" I countered, pointing to the offending spill. He'd spat out the mouthful he'd stolen from my neck, arching it into my foyer like projectile vomit. Then he'd pushed me into it as he rushed to the bathroom and dug about in my cupboard looking for mouthwash. Apparently he'd despised mint for the last three millennia, but one sip of me and he was seeking it out like it was chocolate on day four of a new diet.

"Mix salt and hydrogen peroxide into a paste and leave it on to dry. Then vacuum it off. If you own one, that is," Reginald added, looking around my messed up apartment.

I should have known if anyone knew how to get bloodstains out, it'd be a vampire. Wouldn't want his blazer ruined when he regurgitated a less than perfect tasting meal.

"Have you at least been using the bath salts?" Reginald asked with an exasperated sigh, his pale hand running through his ginger hair.

"It was actual salt!" I yelled. "I don't require seasoning!"

"Here," Reginald said, reaching into his suit jacket with an embarrassed look on his face. Not that I could tell, he didn't exactly have a blood flow to get all flushed on me. "It was perhaps mentioned to me that a human girl may not appreciate my advice, so I bought you something to make amends." He pulled an elegant glass bottle out, the rotound body accentuated by a thousand faceted sides that made it glimmer like a diamond. He held it out to me with his head down, pushing it towards me on his outstretched palm.

"What is it?"

"It is perfume," he announced with a sigh, walking over to put it on my kitchen counter when my awe was not great enough to take it for myself.

I made an effort of shoving myself off the wall to scent the fragrance. "This is rosemary and thyme!" I accused.

"It is a classic combination. I'll leave the applicator too." He plonked a basting brush on the bench.

I studied his face in stunned silence for a moment, looking for any hint this was a joke. He looked deadly serious, provided you overlooked his wispy moustache. And that he always appeared dead.

"Get. Out." I grabbed a clove of garlic and rubbed it over my neck for good measure. For all I knew it made me smell better, his reaction on our first meeting led me to believe I was toxic.

"Bianca," he said with an irritated sigh. "You have a serious health issue. Your blood is not regular, and you should address this before you die an untimely death." He smiled, and flashed his fangs at me. "Well, one I did not devise. Go to sleep young one, next week I'll check if you're tasting better."

He sauntered from my apartment as I checked my heart was still beating. Good, I was alive enough to find myself a new place to live, hopefully somewhere without an undead pest problem. He wanted me to flourish; I'd find out what replanting could do.

"Revelations", by Thomas Clark

1.

"They feed us shit and keep us in the dark."

It was just an ordinary door. All the whitecoats in the basement knew about it. In fact, the mystery of what lay beyond the door was so popular, it was said that late at night, even the walls would whisper.

"You'd think that they'd allow the minds making their new machine a little carte blanche, considering they keep us cooped up down here, starved of sunlight." The subject irked Coleman more than most, a fact he would remind anyone willing to listen.

"Carte blanche?" Avery chuckled. "We don't even know what we're building."

Avery enjoyed this light-hearted, afternoon chat. Their rhetoric had become almost a ritual. But inside he knew that construction wasn't their remit, it was more of a deconstruction, an un-building, akin to the unearthing of a fossil, one gentle brushstroke at a time.

The men continued cycling up the slight incline of the long corridor. Bicycles were standard issue on base, Uncle Sam's contribution to cardiovascular health. The morning descent was simple, but the afternoons were all uphill. In front of them and behind disappeared into darkness. The sensor activated 'light-paths' eerily illuminated only the workers immediate radius.

"Hell, we don't even know how far down here even is," Avery continued, "you know what I'm talking about, you've heard the sounds."

"It's a joke," Coleman said, ignoring the latter comment, "We have higher clearances than that fool up on Pennsylvania Avenue."

"I think the president's too pious to believe a place like this could exist," Avery said, "The briefing would read like a Philip K.

Dick story," and then as an afterthought, "with a dash of Dante maybe."

An automatic door whirred open and the two men idled through and came to a halt at an intersection. Their floor's gradual slope to the main elevator extended before them, but the men's gaze was drawn down, to the deep corridor on their right. It descended perhaps half a mile but it was impossible to tell as there was only one light at the very end of the tunnel; a light which shone down upon a door. It had become another daily ritual in their daily pilgrimage to the surface, to the light. But for a few months ago the tunnel was black, a passage into a void that commanded its own odious reverence, now there was a door, and a guard with earmuffs and an automatic, and a compulsion to know.

With more than a little struggle, the men tore their gaze away and cycled on.

"A little room on nature's floor, without windows, without a door." Coleman broke the silence.

2.

A less healthy part of the men's daily routine was an old watering hole called the 'Proving Ground', a western-themed, refurbished relic that serviced the silver miners of the turn of last century. The gloomy darkness was a welcome contrast to the artificial light of the facility.

"Without windows, without a door ..." Avery mumbled, scratching his head. Coleman laughed as he returned with a fresh pitcher of beer.

"Still ruminating? Thought a smart kid like you'd crack it in no time."

Avery drained what was left of his drink and scowled, "You and your fucking riddles."

"It'll come," Coleman said, leaning back in his chair. "You ever heard of the Stoned-Ape Theory?"

"Does it have something to do with the riddle?"

"It might. Years ago, back when the flower children were just waking up, there were a couple of brothers, whitecoats like us, to a degree, who were doing experiments on their brains. Walls of perception, you know?"

"Acid?"

"Yep. Back when you could get dosed on the government's dime."

"These days they won't even comp our beer," Avery laughed. "Blood out of a stone."

"Anyways," Coleman went on, "these guys postulated that, after the last ice age, when all the shit melted away, our ancestors, homo-something-or-other, came down from the mountains and started to wander on the plains. They began to follow herds of ungulates, eating, amongst other things, a certain fungus that grew on the scat."

"Wildebeest's shit-fungus?" Avery asked, refilling their glasses.

"As the theory goes. This fungus contained a powerful hallucinogen called psilocybin."

"So the apes started tripping?"

"That's right. Apparently the introduction of this chemical into their diet had profound effects on the primates. In a nutshell, over time the synaesthesia, or the blurring of the boundaries between the senses, allowed the development of spoken language, the idea of forming pictures in another's mind through the use of vocal sounds. They then started using tools, forming culture, they began imagining, dreaming."

"Far out."

"Indeed, and that's a good segue to something I've been pondering. You see, a fungus is a perplexing thing. In fact the largest organism in the world is called the honey fungus, grows up in the mountains of Oregon. It measures two and half miles across."

"You've been a closet-botanist this whole time."

"Mycologist. A fungus is actually more closely resembling an animal than a plant, its colonies surviving on waste matter, dead, rotting organic material. It's the same relationship of symbiosis that gave us these big brains of ours."

"Sounds kind of far-fetched."

"Here's where it gets funky. As I'm sure you know fungi reproduce through tiny particles called spores. A fungus will produce a mist of millions of these spores, and they ascend, blowing in the wind. But a spore itself could very possibly survive, under the right circumstances, tens of thousands of years or more, travelling on an asteroid or any other piece of flotsam out there."

"Or jetsam, right? You mean the only reason we're able to have these bouts of philosophising, is some ancient, space-faring spore was lucky enough to find our blue speck of a home?" Avery laughed. "Makes more sense than the bible at least."

"It's in there too. That book's full of occult symbolism. What does Moses see on Mount Saini?"

"God, in a burning bush."

"There's a chemical our brains produce both when we're born and when we die. Again it's a powerful hallucinogenic, that makes the transition more, palatable, I suppose. It's called dimethyltryptamine, it's where we get the term 'tripping' from right?"

"Right, and where does God come into it?"

"God's a metaphor, dig it? DMT's in a lot of things, but the acacia bush has a shit-tonne of it, and burning it is the way to get it out."

"So Moses, like our monkey-forebears, are trippers, and God's a bush? You're sounding like a beat poet."

"That's right man. Moses saw a trans-dimensional being who gave him the skinny on how mankind can be groovy to one another, and he scribbled it down on some stones while off his face."

"So Moses could have just gotten everybody high and he wouldn't have had to have a tantrum and break his tablets?"

"Amen brother."

"What university did you say you went to, Haight-Ashbury?"

"Hallelujah!" This brought on another salvo of laughter.

"Want another hint?"

"No. Wait, what do you mean another hint?" Avery had forgotten all about the riddle.

"Nothing," Coleman grinned.

"Gloat all you like, you've got your own riddle to solve."

"The door," Coleman said, no longer smiling.

3.

Friday afternoon, Avery and Coleman made their usual, trudging ascent. The men rode without speaking. It had been a long day and with each new discovery came a slew of fresh questions.

"You sleep okay last night?" Coleman asked, breaking the silence.

"Hardly. I told you I've been having these dull, throbbing headaches. Well that combined with the beers and your fucking riddle, every time I started to doze off, a little room on nature's floor would pulse behind my eyes."

"Without windows, without a door," Coleman finished absently.

"Indeed. Well, I must have gotten some sleep but it sure doesn't feel like it. You?"

"I got to sleep just fine but it was a bad night. Strange dreams."

"Go on."

"I dreamt I was being buried alive, but I had this feeling, you know, that I wasn't alone; that down there in the black, something was with me."

"Spooky."

Coleman let out a grim laugh. "That ain't even the half of it. I woke up in the desert, about a mile out in the middle of nowhere."

"What the hell were you doing?"

"Digging."

"Digging?"

"Yeah, tore up my hands a treat. When I came to I'd gotten about two feet down."

"You, sleepwalk?"

"Never before last night."

"Jesus."

"I retraced my steps back, the footprints were all close to two yards apart."

"You were running?"

"Yeah, sprinting more like it."

"That is strange. You're lucky not to have broken a leg, or your neck. Hell, you could've gotten fried on a fence, or mistaken for a UFO nut and picked off by one of the hotshots patrolling this place."

"Yeah, lucky. I don't know … if that's the word … I'd … use." Coleman trailed off.

Avery didn't notice, for they had come once more to the crossroads and both men felt the familiar tug of temptation, to make a deal. With who or what they didn't know, nor what bounty might be gained by making the dark road's steep descent, or what must be sacrificed to find out.

"I'm going." Coleman thought aloud, clearly more focused on the former.

From the black, a low thrumming pulsed its ascending harmony, a siren's song, more felt than heard.

"Don't," Avery managed, but Coleman was already gone, sailing down the shaft. The sensor lights rolling on then off, marking his descent, like a torch dropped down a well. Avery's hands tremored, his mind swam. It seemed like madness not to follow, to turn away and let his aching hunger throb. "At least Ulysses was tied to a mast," he thought, longing for a gob of wax to stuff in his ears and silence the sound. Coleman's white silhouette could be seen, tiny, framed by the open door's darkness, then it closed and the shaft went black. At that moment the enchanted harmony tapered, allowing Avery's addled mind reprieve. Somehow he willed himself away and pedalled on.

4.

Much later that evening, Avery again was perched at a corner table of the Proving Ground, sipping scotch with a man with a grey beard and long white hair, a man he only knew as 'Doc.'

"I've heard all sorts of things. Endless caves that feed into caverns that dwarf cathedrals, and the old mining shafts of course." Doc said.

Avery had seen the old man in the elevators of the facility and around the faux-town they called home. He was happy to have someone to talk to and drink with, especially someone who could keep up.

"And then there's the nukes." Doc continued.

Doc was a geneticist. Avery assumed he worked two levels above him, experimenting on god knows what. He had heard stories about the liquid-filled vats and the things they housed, but talk of specifics between the sections was prohibited. Instead, Avery picked Doc's brain about the history of the facility and what lay beneath.

"Nukes?" Avery asked.

"Well, the base is the place, as the old saying goes. The bomb was born here."

"The Manhattan Project, of course, but how does that fit in?"

"After the war they started testing more and more, underground. Much bigger bombs. Seismometers felt them the world over."

"And, so what?"

"Within a millisecond, these contained blasts create a bubble of radioactive gas, millions of degrees in temperature and several million atmospheres of pressure. The surrounding rock is vaporised, forming a large empty space called a 'Melt Cavity'. Russian's call 'em 'Gas Holes.'"

"Rock and roll. How large are these holes?"

"They vary depending on the yield. Most'd be a couple of football fields across, maybe bigger."

"Jesus, we do a lot of these tests?"

"Hundreds, it's like Swiss cheese down there."
Both men drank in silent contemplation.
"Say Doc, you any good at riddles?"

5.

That had been a week ago and Avery had barely slept since. Coleman, the riddle and the door had held his mind prisoner. And here he was again, the crossroads. In days past he had ridden by, looking away, his ears plugged, but the sound found its way in, the experience was torture. The allure of the hum, that rising, rhythmic pulse was hypnotising, even his heartbeat followed it.

Avery must have blacked out or fallen into a trance, because when he came to, he was standing outside the door, his bicycle resting neatly beside Coleman's. He looked back, up the steep path that led into darkness but for a pinhole of light at its apex. He couldn't possibly make it back there, not now. Noticing that Coleman's was gone, he unclipped his bicycle's torch and switched it on. The deep thrum soothed, it assured him that behind the door was the answer his questions. There would be comfort, and he could rest.

As Avery watched his hand turning the knob, part of him realised that the door was different. Not only did it look far older than the sterile, polished whiteness of the rest of the facility, it was covered in splotches of mould. Suddenly the door was closed and he was inside. His beam of light illuminated a spiral staircase descending before him.

After an undiscernible amount of time and depth, Avery made it to the base of the staircase. He at first thought it was just a simple dead-end, then he saw. In the centre of a small square of space was a manhole with its ornate, heavy cover, slid aside. On the cover were inscribed symbols Avery thought to be Sanskrit, but couldn't decipher. A simple ladder disappeared into the darkness of the pipe-like hole, it was impossible to tell how deep it extended.

Another blackout and again he found himself descending, this time the ladder. It was as if he was more and more becoming an observer, watching his actions through the portholes of his eyes. He had no idea of how far down he had gone, but was sweating and his arms ached. After a few minutes, the narrow space around him opened. The sounds became more intense. Avery couldn't see anything but what the torch hanging off his wrist randomly illuminated, acoustically, the place felt immense. As his vision improved, he noticed small pink dots, glowing in the distance below him. "This must be one of those 'Melt Cavities,'" Avery thought.

Again a swathe of time passed and Avery realised he was standing on solid ground. He could see the ladder nearby, lit in a scarlet hue, disappearing upwards. All around him, rising up to a false horizon, were the pink patches. He crouched down and picked up a small piece that grew near his feet. It felt soft, and spongy and wonderful.

"Some kind of Phosphorescent fungus," a distant part of him said, unsurprised how he knew. "A tremendous new truffle, and I'm the pig."

From behind him floated a familiar voice. It was Coleman's, although it sounded gargled, as if spoken underwater.

"Come," it crooned.

Avery imagined that the voice was really in his head but dared not turn around, certain that if he glimpsed the face that spoke those words he would surely die, eternally entombed in this strange place.

"Come … come and see."

Avery realised his hand was attempting to feed his mouth the pink thing and he strained to regain control. His brain bourgeoned, bubbling with madness. All the while the grinding grew, the whispered beckoning continued; a malignant orchestra.

"Come … come and … all the things you'll see."

Time passed, his vision began to improve. Avery realised that he was chewing, swallowing, eating. He watched as a large white shape seemed to appear from a darker area ahead of him. He imagined knew that it was a tunnel leading yet deeper down, also that he was probably hallucinating. The shape got closer and eventually he could see it. An awful, segmented creature with no eyes, larger than a bus. Its translucent skin was mottled with sores and growths. The stench should have overwhelmed him, but didn't. The creature continued over, stopped, then idled back the way it had come.

"Behold a pale … thing." Avery said and laughed absently.

It was no doubt here to guide him further down his path. He could no longer be afraid. He began to follow.

In those final moments, as his individual mind melded into the hive-consciousness of an ancient intelligence, Avery understood everything. He understood his place in the world and the true importance of his work. He saw the majestic complexity of this changing of the guard. It was brilliant. He saw the colonising ships almost two-million years ago, we thought to be asteroids, slamming into earth and countless planets like it, destroying and resetting the life-cycle. With the ships came the spores; catalysts for intelligence and culture of beings. Beings that would flourish, evolving for eons until they reach their zenith; the precipice of creation and destruction: splitting the atom, fission and fusion; tolling the bells that wake the gods.

The inevitability of the formula was all too clear. His was one of the final pieces in this jigsaw of world-seeding. His final moments of being James Lee Avery were pure elation. He realised that not only did he know that the inscription far above him was Sanskrit, it was Oppenheimer's fateful quote from the Bhagavad Gita: I am become Death, the destroyer of worlds; he also finally knew the answer to Coleman's riddle: A little room on nature's floor, without windows, without a door. It was the answer to everything. It was star Wormwood. It was the rising cloud of man's apogee, the smoke signal to herald a new age. It was a mushroom.

"Welcome Swallows", by Bruna Costa

The smell of firewood burning under the cooking stove mingles with that of Grandmother's soup. This room, the only warm room in the house, is where my family hibernates all winter. My three older brothers and my older sister squabble every day. They argue about trivia, like whose turn it is to go outside and collect another bucket of dry dung or an arm full of logs. I'd gladly swap roles with any one of them if I could rid myself of this wheelchair.

I watch everyone going about their daily chores, but in particular, I like to watch Grandfather. His permanent smile, like a crescent moon, is contagious. His eyes sparkle like stars in the night sky. Grandfather sits on his stool and claps and laughs at my siblings and their performances. To him, they are the actors in a live comedy show.

Today, he shuffles across the stone floor, leaning on the broom that supports his bandy legs. He reaches the window on the southern wall. His spindly arms stretch upwards and he unbolts the shutters and pushes against them. But the timber frames are jammed together after months of a bitterly cold winter. He taps them with the broom head until the stiffness abates and he pushes them open. His face beams with pride.

Grandmother pulls her shawl around her. 'Shut that window, you silly old man,' she says. 'That cold air will take us to our graves.'

Grandfather raises a hand to silence her, and then draws the shutters almost to a close. He looks at me with that spark in his grey eyes that warms my heart.

'It's almost time,' he whispers, so that only I can hear. I think he means it's time to greet the new season.

Every day I observe the behaviours around me, and I use the scenes as subject matter for my sketches. Like Grandmother. She leans over the wood stove stirring the pot of unpalatable thick corn soup in one corner of the room. She pulls a loose strand of hair back over her ear and natters about aching joints and noisy children. And Mother, her sleeves rolled up, busies herself at the wash-trough in the opposite corner. She takes her apron and wipes her wet brow, then prods at the boiling laundry with her pole.

'Why don't you stop your whingeing and give my headache a chance to go away,' she says to Grandmother.

'You should discipline your children better. They're the ones that give you a

headache.' The arguments bounce back and forth between them, so I sketch two women working away and add a row of ping-pong balls bouncing from one to the other. Only Grandfather cares to look at my picture and he finds it as amusing as my brothers' karate matches that end up on the floor in a wrestling contest.

Grandfather tells us stories of how he built this house. He always starts with 'sixty years ago,' but by my calculations, his 'sixty' should now be 'seventy' at least. He tells us how he dug stones out of the ground and erected the walls. He fashioned windows and doors from trees he felled in the forest nearby. First, he built this room and a bedroom. After he married Grandmother, he added three more bedrooms for their six sons and two daughters.

The rich land in the Southern China mountain ranges was ideal for growing rice, he says, but it's the remoteness that attracted him here. Our house is one day's trek up the mountain from the nearest town. Grandfather tells us how, single handedly, he levelled out rice terraces with walls around them. They create a pattern of patches down the mountain slope. My brothers ignore his storytelling, but my sister, Jade, and I listen as though we're hearing them for the first time; more out of politeness rather than interest. Mother tells how she and my uncles worked alongside him up to their knees in mud, sowing seedlings in the paddies; how they harvested and threshed the rice, laid it out to dry in the sun and then shovelled it into the storehouse, always under Grandfather's strict supervision.

'We were too young for such hard work,' she says, her voice still bears the bitterness from those early memories. 'You pushed us too hard. That's why all your sons abandoned you.'

'Ah, stop your complaining,' Grandmother says. 'Aren't you following the same footsteps with your children?' It's the only time I hear her defend Grandfather. But her sharp tongue hurt Mother's feelings, and she reminds Grandmother that my brothers were not so young when they first went out to toil the paddies.

Grandmother does not hesitate in blaming Grandfather for our impoverished conditions. She insists he should have built his house closer to the village and blames the isolation for the loss of two of their children. Her youngest baby, a boy, died at birth and is buried in a little grave next to my aunt who perished after an attack of pneumonia. She was twelve. Grandfather planted a cherry tree to mark the spot. I want to believe they help the tree set beautiful blossom so we can reap delicious cherries from it.

My uncles did eventually leave Grandfather's house, but Mother stayed and married Father, the man my grandparents chose for her. She obeyed their wishes and maintained the tradition at the time. Now we fill the empty beds, but I dread the day my brothers and Jade will abandon our home, and me.

My oldest brother is the only one fortunate enough to go to boarding school, so Mother makes us copy his good work from the old exercise books he brings home on school breaks. Five days a week we all do home schooling in this room. Being clever like

Mother, I am expected to help my empty-headed brothers whenever they get stuck on a lesson. But I prefer to rush through my lessons and be the first to have a chess game with Grandfather. The set he hand carved many years ago sits permanently on a little table against the wall. He may be old and frail, but he held the title of champion chess player in our family until I was eight. Then I started beating him. But I suspect it's only because I am the youngest that he lets me win.

This room is where Grandfather and Mother discuss important matters with Father when he is on leave. Mother says she looks forward to the day he will stop going away to work the mines. She smiles at the prospect of him taking charge of the house and the rice growing. But for now, she is too preoccupied to find anything to smile about.

I see this room as our family's beating heart. From my wheelchair, I experience each pulsating moment.

Different seasons bring different activities, and at the end of summer, my brothers harvest the corn that grows on a plot behind the storehouse. Jade and I work side by side, peeling back the husks and stringing bunches of fresh corn together. My brothers scramble up the wooden ladder and straddle each bunch over the horizontal beams. Corn spears form a golden canopy dangling above us like festive decorations. They fill our room with the colour of sunshine for most of the year. When Mother knocks down some cobs with her long stick for our evening meal, Grandfather wittingly pinches a couple and takes them to Grandmother. He tells her to pop some kernels on the stove while he shuffles off into the little storeroom behind the fireplace and returns with the pot of honey. Like an excited bee, he drizzles some honey over the popped corn, and offers everyone a treat, his crescent grin spread across his wrinkled face.

Jade grinds the rest of the dried kernels into flour.

'Grind those kernels finely,' Mother tells her when she complains of aching arms. 'Or Grandmother will be the one complaining.' Coarse pieces usually end up piercing her gums.

'And we will all complain of aching ears,' I say to myself. With the corn semolina, Mother mixes up a batch of delicious savoury pancakes for our evening meal.

When the days grow longer and warmer, Mother and my brothers and Jade leave the house to plough the rice fields and repair the terrace walls in preparation for the new season's rice drop. Grandfather and I wave them off and watch the sun creep up over the mountain peaks.

Cool mist settles on my face before it surrenders to the warmth of the morning rays.

The aroma of rich mountain soil and sweet wet grass mingles with the smell of fresh dung still smoking in the yak's enclosure. Grandfather points out the springs of water trickling down the rocks on the mountain face closest to us. His bent finger points to the tracks up the mountain where he trekked many times looking for bonsai that grew in crevices. Now they flourish in pots that line the wall around our house. He has taught me how to prune his ancient trees and I have sketched them for him.

The eagle calls out and I watch it drift in and out of the clouds high above me. I close my eyes and imagine my body floating out of my chair and onto its back. Together we soar through moist clouds, over tall mountains and deep valleys. The thought of what it sees when flying so high is exhilarating.

I go inside the house intending to draw the eagle and my exhilarating images, but the grumpy one says I'm wasting my time;

that I consume too much paper and wear down too many pencils. Grandfather turns towards me and winks comically before disappearing into the store room. His smile suggests that he is up to some mischief, and that makes my heart sing. He returns with black paint and slender brushes. He is off again and returns dragging a thin board with great difficulty. He says I am to paint their portraits. I paint him first, smiling his cheeky grin, and then I paint Grandmother, complaining as usual. Grandfather laughs at the images. He says he will ask my brothers to hang my artwork on the wall. The grumpy one holds her tongue when she sees herself in my picture and I get to sketch the soaring eagle on paper without the criticism.

Mother displays my sketches at her market stall each month and has sold several already. She says most people prefer my pencil sketches, but she manages to sell some charcoal drawings too. With what she earns, she buys more paper and pencils for me so Grandmother has little to complain about.

When I was little, Mother took my two older brothers to work in the rice fields. Jade stayed home with me. Grandfather says I was inconsolable, that I desperately wanted to go with Mother. So as to pacify me, he carved a figurine of a rice grower, knee deep in mud. I wore it like a pendant around my neck. He has since carved nine more, one for each of my birthdays. I have herons, frogs and dragonflies, each one a replica of creatures that live in the rice paddies and I keep the figurines in my wooden box beside my bed. But my precious rice grower is always with me and I cradle it in my hand when I make my secret wish.

Now that I am older, I help Grandmother chop up vegetables and mend holes in socks while the rest of the family is out working. But my efforts are never satisfactory, and I long for the evenings when the ducks return from foraging in the rice paddies. Then I escape outside and help Grandfather shoo the ducks into the duck house. I toss them their rations of bread and corn kernels before he locks them in for the night. In the mornings, he collects the eggs and places them on my lap. He says we make a great team. However, when the ground is too wet, I don't object any more when Jade takes my place and I watch from the door.

I have not ventured out on wet days since the time I disobeyed the grumpy one and wheeled myself outside. On that day, my wheelchair became bogged, and Grandfather, too weak to drag me out of the sludge, waited with me under the heavy rain until Mother and my siblings returned from the rice fields. The blanket Grandfather held over our heads did not prevent the cold from seeping through our bones and he contracted pneumonia. We almost lost him. I did not need Grandmother's accusations to bear the guilt of what might have happened. Every night I cried myself to sleep and begged a   higher power to let my grandfather live. When he eventually recovered, he carved a picture on a piece of timber that shows the two of us huddled under a blanket in the rain.

He often stares at the plaque and smiles. That tells me he bears no grudges against me.

However, my grumpy Grandmother gives me reason to be anxious, particularly when I overhear a recurring conversation between her and Grandfather.

'You should have put her out in the cold when she was born.' She mumbles thinking I cannot not hear. 'That girl is already ten and still of no use to us.'

I think she must mean my legs are useless.

Grandmother says these things when Father is away in the mines and Mother is out in the fields. At least they do not hear her thoughtless words. Grandfather ignores her, but my chest grows tight from the fear of knowing I will be sent to an orphanage when he is no longer with us. That is, if she has her way.

My secret wish is that he lives forever.

At night, when we retire to our beds, I ignore miserable Grandmother's grumbles and count to ten. By then, Grandfather's loud snores muffle her hurtful threats. I want to believe his noisy rumbles are saying. 'I'm tired of your complaints and don't want to hear any more,' but sadly, Grandmother does not hear what I hear.

Winter is about to leave us. Water from the mountain springs and from constant rainfalls has saturated the rice paddies. Grandfather's anxiety intensifies. Each morning, he pushes the window shutters wide open and gazes out towards the southern horizon. He ignores the cold drifting into our room and leaves the shutters ajar. And he waits. His face lights up on the day two swallows rest on our window sill. It's the sign he's been waiting for.

'Welcome, swallows,' he whispers. 'See. I told you it's time,' he says more loudly.

'Time for what?' Grandmother says, although she knows the answer; we all do.

'Time to sow the rice.'

I clasp my figurine in my hands and share Grandfather's excitement. Mother and brothers prepare the trays to sow rice seed.

Grandfather shuffles around the family room, unable to lift his weary legs. His footsteps falter in the weeks that follow. I watch him toddle back and forth leaning on his broom, stifling his persistent cough. He keeps watch over the swallows that build their muddy nest in their usual corner of our family room. I sketch the birds' progress, their shape and form when they fly, and I draw them dutifully peering out of the nest when it is complete.

I also sketch Grandfather's increasing stoop and notice how he sleeps longer each morning, dozes longer in the day, and retires earlier in the evenings. Although his bed is in the family room now, his cough worsens, and the warm poultices Mother places on his chest cannot shift the stubborn phlegm.

On the day Grandfather refuses to rise from his bed, I hear the baby chicks chirp for the first time. He also hears them, and his crescent smile spreads across his pallid face, only he cannot raise his head.

My heart is heavy with sorrow.

I sketch him lying there, eyes closed, as if asleep. The rise and fall of his chest is barely noticeable beneath the pile of blankets and his puffed up doona. He raises a hand and points to Grandmother. I call her and she comes to his bedside. He whispers in her ear and Grandmother shuffles back to her cooking, mumbling into her handkerchief and wiping away tears.

My brothers race in, feet all muddied from having worked in the rice fields.

'Grandfather, we've filled all your terraces,' they say.

Sadly, Grandfather cannot be woken.

I fumble for my figurine. Warm tears drip down my trembling hands and smudge the sketch on my lap. The happiest years of my life have ended.

Father returns from the mines, for good this time. Grandmother concedes that I should stay home and not go to an orphanage. That was Grandfather's final wish. In return, I promise him I will look after his bonsai.

And so, my heart has good reason to learn to sing again.

♥

"Flight", by Megan Costigan

Inky knew he was special, but he wanted more. He was shy about it, and then ruffled. So many people flipped him the wrong way. Not his owner, she was good. But others, many slipped their left thumb across the middle of his back cover and flipped from back to front. Lately, it bothered him. The back to front business. It meant he stayed on the page. That he didn't get to fly. That wasn't right was it? Flipping him the wrong way forced him backwards into the black square, and not out, flying and free.

Unexpectedly, he began to cry. Inky, hand drawn pigeon from Paris, France, Number 6 Rue de la Folie Mericourt 75011, gasped and sobbed, head dipped deep into his wings. Inky, small but proud participant in the 'On Reflection' flip-book collection, saturated his own crisp white pages. For minutes he cried. He whimpered a little. Then he stopped.

Tipping his head up slowly, Inky fluffed his little wings and sighed, looking out through his pages deep in thought. He shouldn't cry, he had much to be thankful for. The flip-book's cover was a quick, magic orange, his favourite colour, and he was drawn beautifully. Sharp, black ink on crisp white pages. Cute triangular beak, round squat body perched on scratchy legs. Small, discrete wings – three little semi-circles on top of each other – hinting at the possibility of flight.

The book's sequence was thoughtful and straightforward. If flipped correctly, Inky danced across the page from left to right, passed by a simple black square, peeked into it like a mirror, then flew up (like a bird) and off, through the square and away to the right hand corner of the page. Of course, he never really flew off. His body was drawn to carry up through the square and off to the right edge of the page. Then the book finished. He simply returned to the front of the book and rested quietly till he was opened again.

Thankful, he should be thankful. He was glad to be alive and so vibrant, on fresh pages beneath a jaunty orange cover. He was pleased to have snuck into Australia from Paris without a visa and he was pleased he rested here in a warm room with a few occasional visitors.

There was the curious silver tabby cat who sometimes came and sniffed at him and nudged him to the left with his wet nose. Inky wasn't scared by the tabby, he liked the company really. And he was funny for a cat. Sometimes he attacked the shag carpet as if there was a wind-up mouse giving him trouble, then just ran off madly with his ears up and tail all straight. Inky smiled as he remembered. Funny.

Then there was that black dog who came around every now and then. He had visited him last night as a matter of fact, at quite a late hour, just when Inky was feeling a bit low and wanted to be alone. Snuck around the bookshelf and whined until Inky woke up. Only to claim all sorts of nonsense, like that he ate words and punctuation marks for dinner and that his owner was Winston Churchill of all people! A fat black cartoon dog with such a famous owner – Inky knew it was all in the poor dog's head. As for the animal's diet, he couldn't comment – Inky only needed air between his pages to survive not food of any sort. Given his rotund shape, maybe the dog should cut down on the full stops!

Inky giggled to himself and nestled back into his book cover. He drifted off to sleep exhausted, his heart a little heavy, one scratchy foot slipping off the pages to dangle in the air. Occasionally he jerked in his sleep and emitted a soft, snorey coo as he slept. Occasionally a small tear slid down his face and dropped on to the shag carpet.

Morning broke fiercely through the study's curtains and Inky woke with a snap and a tiny shudder. He had overslept. The tabby cast him a sideways glance and wet grin as he waltzed past, belly bulging from a big breakfast and water dripping off one whisker.

Inky threw his leg back onto the pages and stretched. Would he be flipped today he wondered?

He stood up and organised himself, walked back and forth across the pages checking they were fresh and uncreased, looked into his black square and tidied it, made sure it was still sharp and neat. Then he waited.

At ten past three in the afternoon there was action. His owner came into the study, picked the flip-book up and brought him into a room he hadn't seen before. The kitchen he guessed, because there was a large white box that hummed and a metal spout that dripped. Inky settled into the left hand side of the page and waited patiently. He licked his left wing so it settled perfectly and did a little whistle to perk himself up.

His owner touched a silver box and slowly he could hear a tune begin and carry into the air. Opera, he knew immediately, sopranos, and, was that Lakme, the Indian Princess they were singing in duet? His heart beat a little faster. His creator, Jean-Vincent, had played that song as he was being drawn (born)! Oh my goodness, Inky thought. I am a little excited. But there was more to come! His owner walked over to the curtain and pulled it back sharply. Well I never - he could see the sky! The bluest blue blue he could ever imagine filled the window, and wait, was she going to… Yes, his owner reached across and actually slid open the window!

Inky was beside himself and thought his wing might start to twitch or shake or fall off or something equally silly. He tucked it in beside himself firmly and gazed with longing out the window. The sky! But wait, was that…? In a tree outside the window he saw a flutter and whistle, and there, on the thinnest branch, landed a yellow-breasted finch who turned and looked his way! Inky almost fell off his page onto the table. He was as gob-smacked as a black-ink, hand-drawn, flip-book pigeon could be and gave up altogether on his wing which had shot up at an odd angle and was twitching and shuddering like he didn't know what.

Inky took a deep breath and tried to calm himself, but instead, things began to change. He heard the Indian princess duet begin to rise, loud and high, and fill his little ears until his whole body was filled with sopranos. A strong breeze then began through the window and started stirring the cover of his book, lifting it up, fluttering his pages, sweeping things up and down. As the duet rose up and high and down and up, the music filled his body and the breeze swept in roughly and the sun broke into the room and started burning his squat, round body and the duet continued and the breeze swept his pages over and shook him out of his book madly so he tumbled onto the table!

A hot glow of yellow covered and bathed him and the opera rose him up off the table and into the glow and the breeze and the sun and the blueness started surrounding him and the duet peaked and carried him into the orange and the yellow and the breeze blew him towards his black square which appeared before him but in the air not on the page and the opera swept him towards it while his book flew madly up and fell away through the air beside him and the yellow and the orange and the breeze lifted him up and straight through the black square and off to the right and away into the blue and breeze and burnt him into the opera of when he was born and up and out of his very own real window into the sky and the orange and the yellow and the crisp fresh blue and he rose up and away and flittered and skittered and danced and laughed and cried and sketched and flew into the universe's air, her love, her body.

Inky   was   free.

"Hand Me Down", by Leonie Crowden

On Sophie's bedroom wall was a decorative plaque that read:

> *'Dance like there's nobody watching,*
> *Love like you'll never be hurt,*
> *Sing like there's nobody listening,*
> *And live like it's heaven on earth.'*
> *- William W. Purkey*

Like a mantra providing advice on her life's direction, this was exactly what this special little girl did; danced, sang and lived her life completely to her own tune.

Like most typical little girls, Sophie was besotted with the colour pink, knew all the lyrics to her favourite songs and movie soundtracks and loved to dance. She also happened to have Down syndrome but that was the least typical thing about her.

Most people have forty-six chromosomes in their genetic makeup. Sophie had forty-seven. This extra piece of DNA meant that her growth and development had been slower than most children. Having the physical attributes typical of children with Down syndrome - a round face, flat nose, tiny ears and almond shaped eyes, these same distinctive features also made Sophie unique. Being only a small part of who she was, Down syndrome didn't make her any less valuable a human being. Not perceiving herself as any different from anybody else, Sophie just wanted to be treated the same as any other child, worthy of all the love, acceptance and respect deserving of every human being.

From the moment her mother, Rachael knew she was pregnant again, she and her husband, Nick, experienced an overwhelming love for their unborn child. They spent the next seven months creating an image of their baby, marvelling at the tiny miracle that would soon complete their family. Neither predicted that her arrival would send their whole universe spinning on its axis,

causing them never to look at the world in quite the same way again.

When Sophie arrived bearing little resemblance to her sisters, everyone joked that she'd been delivered by the milkman. However, in quieter moments, Rachael's maternal instincts told her that she was different in more ways than just her physical features. On the second day of her life, when the parents were told that their baby had Down syndrome, their innate protectiveness immediately went into overdrive; those moments forever etched into their memory.

Rachael and Nick clung to each other, frozen as time appeared to stand still. With their minds in turmoil, swirling with confusion, anxiety and terror at what lay ahead, they tried to process the devastating news. Neither one spoke. There were no words to say. This wasn't how it should've been. It was a birth, not a funeral. There should've been cameras clicking, jubilation and celebration. Instead there was silence, despair and desolation.

However, as they nursed their baby and gazed into her eyes, they were consumed by an unconditional love for their daughter. Their innocent child hadn't asked to be born with a disability. She wasn't damaged goods to be returned for a refund because of imperfection or failing to meet expectations. As desperate tears flowed from the depths of their souls, so too did an in intense, absolute love that would drive them to protect their precious child above all else.

It's amazing how the direction and purpose of life can irrevocably change in a matter of minutes but as fierce parental instincts were unleashed, Rachael and Nick knew that their child needed them. Suddenly, from among the many feelings eddying within, other emotions surfaced – love, certainty and hope. They'd just delivered a gorgeous baby daughter. She was a part of them, with her father's dimples, her mother's fair complexion and the most beautiful almond eyes. She just happened to have an extra chromosome, that's all.

Rachael and Nick had two choices – either collapse in a heap and ask themselves, "Why us?" or consider their situation from a different perspective and ask, "Why not us?". Sophie was their child. They were her parents and she needed them, so they made their pledge. Fiercely determined that their daughter would enjoy the same opportunities as their other two children and that she'd live a fulfilling life, filled with good health, happiness and respect, they vowed to do everything within their power to eradicate any impediment that might prevent Sophie from reaching her full potential.

There was a time when Rachael and Nick had known very little about children with Down syndrome. Like many people, they'd considered them lethargic, incoherent, incapable and unable to contribute anything positive to society. How totally wrong Sophie proved these misconceptions to be. Even though at times they were reminded by people who looked at them with pity and made callous comments, Rachael and Nick soon began to forget Sophie had Down syndrome. When they looked at their daughter they saw a sweet, loving child, who melted their hearts with her love and gentleness so instead of their 'Down syndrome baby', they began to refer to her as their 'baby with Down syndrome' hoping that people would stop viewing her diagnosis and begin perceiving her as a child who just happened to have particular needs.

As she grew older it became more obvious that negative perceptions surrounding people like Sophie were preventing her from enjoying the same opportunities as her siblings. Rachael and Nick were determined to fight for her acceptance within society. With a family of daughters, dance was a big part of their lives. Her two sisters attended dance classes so it was only natural that Sophie would want to follow them. However, as classes became more structured and competitive, the teacher informed them that she couldn't continue. Sophie was shattered and so were her parents. How do you tell a child that she's not good enough; that she no longer meets the requirements? How do you tell a child that because she's different, she has to stop doing the one thing she loves? In her eyes there was no difference. In her eyes she was just who she was, Sophie, and she struggled to understand why she was being denied the one thing she loved with such passion.

However, parental love knows no boundaries. Telling Sophie she could no longer attend dance classes stirred up primitive protective instincts in her parents. They became tenacious in their determination to ensure that their daughter could continue doing something that gave her so much pleasure and satisfaction. If Sophie could no longer be taken to classes, they'd bring the classes to her. Spurred on by her daughter's constant insistence that she could teach her and with only her experience as a 'Dancing Mother', Rachael decided to establish dance classes for children like Sophie. Together, she and Nick secured a venue and through networking with families of children with Down syndrome they advertised classes.

The first session arrived with Rachael questioning the sense of her ambitious actions but the expression of pure delight on Sophie's face soon quelled her nerves, providing her with the courage to forget her own inhibitions and to start viewing life through the freshness and innocence of her daughter's eyes. Trembling with nerves as she watched the babble of families arriving, Rachael noticed that it was only the parents who displayed any apprehension. Each child's face glowed with an excited flush and a contagious eagerness which soon spread throughout the room. Before long everyone was laughing and smiling. Parents relaxed as they saw the sparkling eyes and delighted faces of their children; their obvious enjoyment generated by the opportunity to express themselves freely without fear of judgement or rejection.

At the end of the session, Sophie threw herself into her mother's arms, quivering with excitement as tears streamed from her beautiful almond shaped eyes and rolled down her cheeks. Locked in a precious moment in time, mother and daughter clung to each other absorbing the other's joy; their body language expressing the raw emotion bubbling within their souls.

The first class was a resounding success and cemented the foundation for what would become an integral part of the lives of many children and their families. At first there was only a handful of participants but word soon spread throughout the community and before long several dozen children were attending regularly. Families began travelling considerable distances each week and as the children's confidence blossomed, so did Rachael's. After several months, she and Nick realised the necessity to formalise classes, so they registered as a business, set up a governing committee of enthusiastic parents and became an endorsed charity.

In those early days, Rachael could never have imagined how incredibly rewarding it would be to witness these children expressing themselves through the love of dance. With the starkness of the hall transformed into a kaleidoscope of sound, colour, laughter, energy and joy, children, with sequinned costumes sparkling and faces beaming, twirled around the dance floor, sashaying in time to the music.

Transported to another all inclusive world where everyone was accepted, parents soon forgot their children's limitations. Revelling in the opportunity to showcase their sons and daughters in a different light, they watched as their children flourished within the security of a nurturing, non-threatening environment. As they marvelled at the dancers' achievements, they were drawn into the magic of the miracle unfolding before them.

A total lack of inhibition allowed Sophie and her fellow dancers the freedom to interpret the music with an honesty and vitality that was refreshing and uplifting. Unencumbered by the constraints of self consciousness or pre-conceived expectations, they danced from the heart; their innocent transparency allowing anyone watching the chance to glimpse into their souls and witness the pure joy emanating from deep within. Watching them dance was like witnessing the dawning of a new day. As they twirled around the dance floor, their sunny smiles illuminating the room, their faces shone with the warm golden glow of happiness, their eyes sparkled like fresh dew drops and there was a clarity and freshness to their movements which held the promise of future possibilities.

With the opportunity to express themselves through their love of dance, these children were improving fitness levels, developing self esteem, boosting confidence and blossoming physically, intellectually and emotionally. Thanks to generous local media coverage, their annual concerts began to attract large audiences and along with their performances at special events, these children were refuting many misconceptions surrounding Down syndrome, as they spread awareness within the community to educate people and change attitudes.

When she was born Rachael and Nick had found it hard to imagine their future living with a child like Sophie. Now they couldn't imagine their world without her. She'd given her parents many challenges and extra responsibilities but her boundless love and joy had also enriched their lives in ways they never thought possible. Her enthusiasm and exuberance had given Rachael the strength to step outside her comfort zone and do something important for those who can't stand up for themselves. She'd shown her parents that, with the correct learning environment and opportunities, people with special needs can contribute positively to society. She'd taught them humility and compassion and made them more patient and accepting of others. They'd learnt to view the world through Sophie's eyes to see that life's successes aren't quantified by material possessions but by love and personal achievement.

With the loving support of her family, this delightful child had shown the world that, rather than weathering the storm, it's possible to learn to dance in the rain. Sophie, who just happened to have Down syndrome, was proof that although we can't select the music life plays for us, we can certainly choose how we dance to it as she continued through her life to

'Dance like there's nobody watching,
Love like you'll never be hurt,

Sing like there's nobody listening,
And live like it's heaven on earth.'

"Break On Through", by Richard Cusack

I freeze as the big Harley mounts the sidewalk and comes charging straight at me.

Spinning on my heels, I leap over the kerb and take off down Mulholland like a complete maniac. A few seconds later a blue Corvette slams to a halt nearby.

The driver gives me a cheeky grin. "Where you headed, pal?"

"Anywhere but here, mate."

"Jump in. Mojo's the name."

"G'day, I'm John."

"Okay, Johnny boy. Let's get ourselves a drink."

Gunning the engine, Mojo drives to a motel on Santa Monica Boulevard. I get out of the car and follow him up a flight of stairs into a small apartment with graffiti on the walls. Mojo points me towards a battered old sofa. Then he opens a pint of bourbon and proceeds to pour half of it down his throat

"Welcome to my humble abode, Johnny boy," he says, passing me the bottle.

"Been here long, Mojo?" I ask, taking a slug.

"Too long my friend. So what's an Aussie boy like you doing in L.A.?"

"I'm an actor. And stop calling me boy, will you?"

Mojo sings a song about riders on a storm. He's got a nice baritone. Sharp threads too: snakeskin boots, a leather jacket and a conch belt inlaid with silver and fancy gemstones. His face looks vaguely familiar.

"Do I know you from somewhere?" I ask him.

"You do now. Getting any work round these parts?"

"I couldn't get arrested at the moment."

"Hang with me and you will," Mojo snorts. "You remind me of Tom Baker. He was a hungry young actor too."

"Look Mojo, I've tried real hard to---"

Mojo holds up his hand. "Relax, pal. It'll come."

I bite my lip as the Harley-Davidson rumbles by outside.

"You're on the run," Mojo observes. "What's the story?"

"Well, I was rooting this chick when a Hell's Angel walked in on us. Turns out she was his old lady."

Mojo roars with laughter. I don't see the funny side.

"Feeling poorly, Johnny?" he asks with concern.

"A little…"

Mojo lights up a joint. "Here, this'll level you out."

"Thanks."

Mojo shakes his head. "Hey, even I never balled an Angel's lady."

"Give it a go, old man."

"And how old are you, smartass?"

"Nearly thirty…"

"Try twenty," Mojo growls. "And don't lie to me again."

"Sorry."

Mojo winks right back at me. "Break on through, Johnny boy."

I light a smoke and watch Mojo go to work on the bourbon. Despite his pot bellyand scruffy beard, I can still imagine how he must have looked back in the day.

"It's always today," Mojo says unexpectedly. "Don't you know that, son?"

"Well, yeah…but…are you psychic or something?"

Mojo chuckles softly. "Come on, there's people I want you to see."

We go down to an apartment at the end of the landing. The smell of dope hits me as I trail Mojo through the open door. Candles and incense make the place nice and cosy. A chick with bad skin and feathers in her hair sits on a divan next to a skinny black dude with a guitar.

Mojo bows theatrically. "Johnny, meet Pearl and the Maestro."

Maestro strums out a three cord salute. Pearl jumps to her feet and kisses me smack on the mouth. "You're pretty," she purrs. "Are you Mojo's kid brother?"

Mojo nods approvingly. "Yeah, I guess you could say he is."

Pearl breaks out the booze and a heap of blow. Then we get treated to a hot little concert. The Maestro plays the freakiest shit I've ever heard and Pearl sings right along. She can really belt it out.

I look around and notice a guy with dirty blond hair slumped in the corner. He's flourishing a cigar and sobbing away like there's no tomorrow.

"Who's that bloke?" I say, poking Mojo in the ribs.

"Oh, that's Brian. Poor dude just got canned from the Stones."

Suddenly the room fills with a blinding white light. For a moment I feel like I'm floating in space with beings from another world. Too much blow I guess.

When the concert's over, Pearl starts handing out tabs of acid. I'm keen to indulge, but Mojo puts his foot down. "None for Johnny, he's high enough."

"You're one to talk," Pearl sneers at him.

Mojo grabs a bottle and smashes it against the wall. Everyone falls silent until the Maestro breaks the tension with a beautiful guitar solo. Then Mojo gets the giggles and comes out with some crazy bullshit about being possessed by the spirit of a dead Indian Chief.

Pearl and the Maestro look like they've heard it all before. As they chat together, Mojo bolts outside and climbs up on the balustrade

"I am the lizard king," he yells. "I can do anything."

Pearl shoots me a nervous look. "Johnny, please get him out of here."

Staggering from the room, I haul Mojo to the ground and hustle him back to the apartment. Mojo gets himself a beer and goes off to sulk in the corner

I approach him warily. "You shouldn't have done that, mate."

"Listen, son, if it wasn't for me you'd be dead meat right now."

"Hey, I was only trying to---"

"Don't ever tell me what to do," he shouts, storming out the door.

A couple of hours later, Mojo returns with a six-pack and a fresh bottle of bourbon. He cuffs me lightly on the shoulder. "Okay, Johnny boy?"

I flip him the finger.

"Sorry about before." Mojo lowers his eyes. "I get a little crazy when my pals don't pay me attention."

"You can't always get what you want."

"Wow, that's original," Mojo replies sarcastically.

"I should have let you fall off that bloody balcony," I retort.

"Wouldn't be the first time, buddy."

"Is that right?" I say, cracking a beer.

"Sure is bro'." Mojo sits down with a sigh. "Now let me tell you some things."

Over more drinks and a joint or two, Mojo regales me with outrageous tales of rock 'n' roll debauchery. He's quite the raconteur, but his voice sounds a bit sad. Maybe he knows those days are gone forever.

Later on I get sleepy and stretch out on the sofa. Covering me with a blanket, Mojo goes over to the window and stares out at the bright lights of the Strip.

He looks so lonely I can taste it.

"Goodnight, Mojo," I say, pulling the blanket over me. "Thanks for everything."

"Sleep tight, Johnny boy."

When I awake its daylight and the birds are singing outside. I get up off the sofa and see a roll of cash sitting on the lounge room table. Mojo's boots and clothes lie in a neat pile on the floor. I guess it's his way of saying goodbye.

Changing into Mojo's gear, I pocket the cash and leave the apartment. Halfway down Santa Monica Boulevard I drop into Barney's for a drink. It's about midday and the place is nearly empty. A well-dressed blonde gives me the eye as I approach the bar.

"What'll it be?" says the grizzled barman, watching me closely.

"Double Jack," I reply, giving him twenty bucks. "Got a problem, mate?"

"You look like someone I used to know."

"And who would that be?"

"That would be Mojo, otherwise known as Jim Morrison, lead singer of The Doors."

"You're shitting me."

The barman shakes his bald head solemnly. "Matter of fact Mojo died this very day forty years ago. Sure was sad how they all went like that."

"What do you mean?"

"Well, first Jimi Hendrix OD-ed. Man, could he play guitar. Then Pearl kicked the bucket. That's Janis Joplin case you don't know. Then Mojo signed out. Oh and don't forget Brian Jones. Now he was a strange cat, let me tell you."

I take a drink and think back on the events of the previous day. I'm starting to put the pieces together when the blonde comes up and introduces herself.

"Hi, I'm Kate Sampson."

"John Beaumont," I say, looking her over.

Kate Sampson is the hottest director in Hollywood.

"You're Australian, right?" Kate chirps.

"Too right, love," I say, laying it on thick.

"Can you act?"

"That's why I'm in L.A."

Kate gives me her card. "I like your style. Call me and we'll arrange a test."

When Kate leaves I order a cognac to celebrate my good fortune. Then I look into the mirror directly behind the bar.

Mojo winks right back at me.

Break   on   through,   Johnny   boy.

"Spirit of the Earth", by Pamela Jeffs

The air like the earth was dry. Thirsty. I dropped my shovel and walked back to patch of shade that lingered beneath the spindly limbs of John's gum tree. I sat down on the rock that I had positioned next to his gravestone, picked up my saddle pack and dug about until I found my water flask. I unscrewed the top and held it to my parched lips.

The water was warm and tasted slightly salty. Bore water always tasted like that. John had told me it was mineral salts leaching from the ground that did it. He had been clever in knowing about things like that. Maybe it was because unlike me, he had grown up in a big, far-away city, had gone to school and had learned to read. I had grown up with only my father on the station. For the last twenty years, he had taught me to read landscapes, weather patterns and animal tracks, but there had never been much time for written texts.

"It's bloody hot out in that sun, John. You'd better like this garden when I'm done." I glanced at his gravestone. Dappled patterns of sunlight filtered down through the leaves above to dance across the pale-pink sandstone block. The outline of the image I had carved on it, stood out in sharp relief. It wasn't an exact likeness to his profile but it was the best I could do. I knew he wouldn't mind. He had told me he liked my drawings of him even when they hadn't been perfect. I sighed, wishing that he were still here. I missed our conversations.

A hot breeze fanned its way from across the dry creek bed beyond. I felt the sweat on my skin dry, making it feel taught. The same breeze made Gus, my horse, snort from his place by the tree. With his nose cleared, he shifted his weight onto to his other leg, tilting a back hoof in idle repose as he resettled.

A small whirly–whirly kicked up suddenly in the sun-drenched basin of the creek. It skipped and danced across the cracked clay, spinning a handful of dried leaves and grass upwards as it went. I smiled to myself watching as it tracked crazy patterns across the earth.

My father would have said that the whirly-whirly meant that evil spirits were close by. He was superstitious when it came to the old aboriginal legends. But not me; I saw beauty in the whirly-whirly, beauty in the landscape that it belonged to. That is why I had chosen this place by the creek for John. It was where I would like to be buried when my time came. Still, I could hear his voice in my head, questioning —

"It's a lovely place you picked for me Jane, but why the garden?"

I could just see him, cocking his tousled blonde head and rolling those laughing green eyes of his at me. I smiled wider at the thought, my bottom lip cracking as I did so. I licked thoughtfully at the blood that beaded to the surface and then chuckled out loud. I was certain he would have thought me crazy.

But then again, John hadn't been one to value the importance of little things like I did. Perhaps in being an RAAF pilot and having witnessed the true scale of the world, his eye had only ever been drawn to the extraordinary. It wasn't surprising, coming as he had from the modern part of this 1930's world; a part filled with the likes of airplanes, ever growing cities and man-made gardens.

My world was one of cattle, red earth and blue sky. I had never seen any of those other things, especially gardens like he had described. He had often spoken of his mother's garden in Darwin and how it had been the only place that had ever really felt like home.

"*A green place of solemn beauty,*" he had called it.

Here in my land of red dust, silver bark and dusty green trees, I think he missed that garden most of all. I think he knew he was dying and would have liked to see it one last time. But it was not to be. The injuries from the plane crash that saw him stranded here with us were more than I had the skill to heal. In our short time together though, we had become friends. In fact, he had been the first real friend I had ever had. Building this garden for him was my way of saying both thank you and goodbye.

I glanced down at the few wilted plants that I had carefully gathered for the job. Wattle tree saplings, Sturt's Desert Peas and a trailing vine of jasmine that I had pilfered from behind the cattle yards. They sat waiting; their roots bundled in dampened strips of canvas. I sighed, they seemed a far cry from the flowers John had described but they were to me the very best the drought stricken heart of Australia had to offer.

I screwed the lid of the water flask back into place and sat it on the ground next to my sitting rock. "Back to work," I said.

I got to my feet and re-adjusted the brim of my hat. I reached down and picked up the box of small plants that awaited their new home. They seemed so small but I knew there was moisture in the ground near the creek, even if the water didn't flow along the top anymore. Hopefully it would be enough to see them flourish.

I walked over, kneeled down next to the shovel and set the box to one side. I dug my fingers into the red earth. It was dry and powdery at the top but I felt the moisture below. I unwrapped the delicate roots of each plant and placed them into the holes I had made. It didn't take long to settle them in and press the soft earth back firmly over their bases. I sat back on my heels and looked at my work. They were a motley array of plants but I thought them beautiful in any case.

I dusted my hands clean and got to my feet. I went to grab the shovel but something made me pause.

I looked out across the dried creek bed to the scattered trees and dried Mitchell grass that lined the opposite bank. Something felt different. My shovel had not moved, the whirly-whirly still danced and the cicadas still chirruped; but there was a sense of expectancy in the air – a stillness that existed without the absence of sound.

Then the whirly-whirly subsided.

A twig snapped behind me.

I turned so quickly that a cloud of red dust dislodged itself from the brim of my hat. My gaze fell upon the sitting rock.

It was no longer empty.

A tiny man, if you could call him that, sat crouching on the rock. Beneath the kangaroo fur smock he wore, his skin was silver and scaled like a lizard's. His wide dark eyes stared at me from beneath a bedraggled mop of blue-black hair. His nose wrinkled as he sniffed at me and I noticed a scattering of ochre and white dots painted across the bridge of it. The pattern reminded me of the one on the boomerang my father had hanging in the living room at home.

"What are you doing?" His voice was husky, sounding like the whisper of wind over stone.

"Building a garden," I replied, too shocked to do anything but answer.

The little man leaned over to look at my work. He raised a scaled eyebrow, "This is a garden?"

I glanced back at the plants and suddenly felt embarrassed. Before I had thought how beautiful they looked but now saw them for what they were —a pathetic row of seedlings that in all honesty probably wouldn't survive. I turned back and squared my shoulders, ignoring the sarcastic grin that split the little man's face in half. "I don't need your approval. Go away."

The little man jumped off the rock, his bare feet landing in a cloud of dust. He sauntered up to the plants with his hands locked together behind his back. He bent at the waist and sniffed at them. He shook his head and swiveled his eyes up to meet mine. "These do not belong here," he said.

I felt my anger rising.

"No, not at all," he continued. "The wind chose elsewhere for them to grow. They must be taken back to where they came from."

"This land belongs to me. I will do what I want with it."

The little man's eyes glittered like two chips of obsidian. "Land does not belong to one," he said, "One belongs to it."

I was done listening. I leant over picked up the shovel and leaned it across my shoulder. "The garden stays," I said. "I'll be back to check on it. I wouldn't do anything to try and ruin it, if I were you." I turned away, heading over towards Gus who sat with his ears pressed forward in abject interest of the man.

"Wait," called out the little man after me. "I will help to make it better."

I stopped and turned. I wanted the best for John. "What did you have in mind?"

The little man smiled, an evil little grin. "A Dreaming Flower," he said.

"A what?"

The little man pulled his hand out from behind his back. A shiny red seed lay nestled in the tiny cradle of his palm. "A flower to hold memory," he said. "Put your memories into the seed, plant it and it grows. Memories make the colour; each flower is unique. It's bush magic."

Bush magic? I didn't trust him, but there was something compelling about the seed. It glittered so brightly sitting in his palm, as if it were transparent and the sun itself shone out from its ruby heart.

I was suddenly kneeling in the dirt reaching out for the seed.

Just as my fingers made to close over it, the little man snatched it back to his chest. I stifled a cry of dismay.

He smiled again. "Plant it by your friend's grave."

He was right. I nodded and got back to my feet. I walked out of the broad sunlight and again into the shade. I sat down on the sitting rock.

"Now put your memories in." The little man nodded encouragingly as he dropped the seed into my hand.

The seed felt hot against my skin. Searing almost. I wrapped my fingers around it and closed my eyes, thinking of John. I put his kind smile into the seed, and my enjoyment of the conversations we had shared on the old verandah. I put the memory of how his hair glistened like spun gold in the sun and the way that his eyes crinkled when he laughed. I steered away from the memories of his last few days, the smell of his gangrenous leg, the grey tinge to his skin and the helplessness of knowing that real doctors were too far away to help him.

Suddenly I felt the seed move in my hand. It twitched with life and then to my horror, I felt it bury into my skin. I opened my hand but the seed was gone. There was no blood but I could feel it moving through my hand and up my arm towards my heart.

"What's happening?" I screamed at the little man.

He just stood there, his face grim. "I am a Spirit of the Earth, I belong to this land," he said, "And now, so will you."

I tried to reply but my tongue was tied. My limbs jerked out wide as pain coursed through my body, almost unbearable. In horror, I watched my fingers change. Each one became a petal, dark blue spotted with white. My palms turned bright orange and filled with pollen, each becoming the heart of a flower. A glistening red seed burgeoned suddenly into existence, cocooned in the core of each one.

My body lengthened and I felt my feet dig into the ground. My toes became roots and I felt them burrow deeper and deeper into the earth. With them, I tasted moisture; I tasted mineral salt; I tasted the dead timber of John's coffin.

Before my eyesight failed, I saw myself reflected in the dark orbs of the little man's eyes. I had become a flowering tree; more unique and twice as striking than anything I had ever seen. I tried to cry out but no sound came. My hearing faded last, the final sound that of the little man's voice.

"Beautiful," he whispered, as I felt him pluck the red seeds from   my   palms.

"Listen. Remember.", by Christine Johnson

For Mei Si, one of Grandmother Ying Mei's greatest strengths was that she never stopped telling stories of the past, stressing their significance for the future. Even in the twilight of her life, she continued to dream dreams.

As Mei Si's marriage day approached she prompted her Grandmother each day, inwardly counting how little time she had left at home before becoming a bride. Grandmother Ying Mei recalled her own lifetime for her granddaughter - adding in words of astute advice here and there.

'Always listen. Remember what those with know-how choose to tell you, even if it seems insignificant. For at some point in the future, you'll ask what it was like. Question how it was done. Or wonder why did it come to be? And it is then, if your chance has passed, you'll look back. Wish you had been more compliant.'

Counselled in this way, Mei Si and Grandmother Ying Mei, although they would be divided once the young woman married, remained close in affection and understanding.

Despite years, Grandmother Ying Mei's ability to remember remained picture-perfect. Every story she told began in the same way.

'Listen. Remember.'

How Grandfather Chang started his working life as a cloth seller and hawker of thread. Hardly a lucrative or secure occupation, but it was all he had. He may have moved on to other work in time, if a marriage had not been arranged for him to a young woman with other ideas. The girl Ying Mei, despite her name, was neither flower-like nor enchanting. As a scrawny teenager the skin on her face bore livid scars of boils that plagued her as a small child. There had been times when her father, financially desperate, looked at this daughter, mulling over whether the custom of trading girl-children for a little profit was such a bad thing. But he had put the thought aside, and persevered.

Grandmother Ying Mei's eyes twinkled as she recollected.

How she was a proud, strong-willed young woman, used to putting up with the taunts of others from an early age. Considered by many in her village fortunate to marry even a lowly hawker like Chang, like many girls she was forced into marriage; just thirteen when her mother told her of the arrangements made by the matchmakers.

Ying Mei, with characteristic bluntness, had asked, 'Why?'

'Because your father has decided,' answered her mother.

'Why?'

Knowing this pattern could repeat itself for some time if a fuller explanation was not provided, Ying Mei's mother pointed out her daughter should be pleased.

'You are the eldest girl. You must be sent out in marriage. Clear the way for your younger brothers to receive wives, further their careers and carry on the good name of their father.'

This explanation made no sense to Ying Mei whatsoever. Why should her life be sacrificed to accommodate her brothers' ambitions?

'I don't want to be married. Anyway, this man you speak of, when he sees my ugly face he will not want me for a wife!'

'He has no interest in your face, girl.'

With that her mother turned away. The conversation closed.

And, for all her lack of physical charms, the young Ying Mei proved a good match for Chang, a good match for a hawker of thread. She had youth, a driving energy and an ability to make the most of a poor lot. Not that life was easy. From the first, it was plain she married a man struggling to keep a roof over his head and feed himself. Let alone keep a wife.

Grandmother Ying Mei described to granddaughter Mei Si what it was like.

How her limited, childlike understanding of what being a wife entailed came from observing her parents. She heard stories of girls given in marriage being beaten brutally by their husbands, but she had never seen her father inflict any sort of cruelty upon her mother. Although whenever a new baby was about to arrive, she was told to keep away. Then she heard her mother screaming; groaning and panting in agony, like an animal. Now married, the young Ying Mei was determined nothing like this would ever happen to her.

How, terrified on the first night after her wedding, she spat and scratched like a stray cat when Chang approached her. A decent enough man, in the end he simply laughed.

'Ai-ya! Well, we have plenty of time, little one. And at least my new wife is fighting fit!'

He laughed again, shaking his head at her ferocity, then rolled over and slept. Ying Mei remained awake, sitting up with arms locked around her knees, keeping watch and shivering with fright. She did not trust him.

'He'll grab me and overpower me if I close my eyes.'

That is what she thought. Eventually, tiredness overcame her. Nodding once, twice, her head fell forward. Her body relaxed. She passed a first night in her new husband's bed huddled under a coarse blanket, plagued by strange dreams.

How for one more night Chang remained patient. Assuring her he just wanted to touch her, but would do no more. Grandmother Ying Mei took Mei Si back in time. There she lay. A young wife unyielding and tense, as his clumsy hands explored her lean body. He lifted her small, wrapped feet one at a time, fondling them. The handling left behind a prickly sensation, as if miniature spiked insects burrowed into her and crawled along under her skin. The feeling lasted long after he had desisted.

How, on the third night, Chang took her hand in his. When she resisted he tightened his grip, moving her hand down between his legs. Ying Mei felt the heat of him, was shocked by his hardness. Before she could struggle against what was happening, Chang's body arched and tightened. He moaned. Ying Mei felt a warm wetness dripping out between her fingers. Thinking it must be blood, her stomach lurched. Chang released her. Panicking, she tottered out of bed, pressing her spine against the flimsy wall. But then in the darkness, she heard a different sound. Straining to make it out, Ying Mei realised. Chang was laughing.

'Ai-ya, you see little one! Hsiao tsai tzu, you young animal! All will be well. Now come back to bed again, where it is warm.'

With that he turned onto his side and was soon asleep. Ying Mei crawled in beside him. Exhausted, she too fell into a restless sleep.

Grandmother Ying Mei reminded her granddaughter Mei Si how custom allowed a return home to visit family at a set time after marriage. But she spoke to no one about what went on in the dark between herself and her husband.

It was an eagle-eyed aunt in Chang's family who eventually took her to one side. Although it had become mutely established between Chang and his wife that at night Ying Mei would mostly succumb to her husband's wishes, the match was still not fully consummated. Chang's aunt suspected as much. Kindly, she explained to the girl the full nature of her wifely duties. How she must not anger the gods.

'Remember. Before anything, Chang is your husband now. To be followed and obeyed. It is not his fault he has the nature of a man.'

'But I did not ask to share his bed,' Ying Mei countered stubbornly.

For a moment Chang's aunt almost smiled. It was then she gave the young Ying Mei a small white figure of Kuan Yin, Goddess of Mercy.

The same one Grandmother Ying Mei carried close to her all these years later and now showed her granddaughter Mei Si, quoting exactly the same advice.

'Listen and remember. More belongs to marriage than four legs in a bed. Sharing a bed is not all there is to life. People grow different dreams in the same bed.'

Chang's aunt pointed out her nephew's habits suggested he was likely to be kind, certainly a man of simple needs; not forcing his desires upon her, as she expected.

'He could have,' Chang's aunt explained. 'And he might have seen to it you were ridiculed and shamed, humiliated, sent back to your family. Instead he has bided his time, been prepared to wait.'

Chang's aunt indicated the little statue of Kuan Yin.

'Heed the word of the Goddess. Open your heart to radiate love, so that love can come back to you.'

Fearful, Ying Mei steeled herself the next time her husband made advances. Lying still, not pulling away from him. Aware of the change, Chang spread her legs, placing her little feet encased in their bed slippers behind his back. She gasped at the stabbing sensation. The whole business was over in seconds. And this time her husband did not laugh. Instead he sighed deeply and fell onto his back, murmuring gently into the darkness.

'Chen hao, you are very good, my little one! Sleep now, my little wife, my pretty wife.'

Within moments he was dead to the world. She listened to his breathing. Her neck and cheeks flushed with an unexpected rush of warmth. Ying Mei lifted her hand to touch the uneven skin on her scarred face.

No one had ever said she was pretty before.

Mei Si's marriage day was here. After a day of ritual and ceremony, the bridegroom she had never seen would take her away. Carried off in a curtained sedan chair, firecrackers set alight in the street to ward off evil spirits. Through these last nervous hours she remembered Grandmother Ying Mei's storytelling.

How, coming to terms with what was happening to her at night, the young Ying Mei started to feel at home in her new life during daylight hours. Her husband's goods, simple cloth and threads in the eyes of others, she began to see as things of greater potential.

How until now her hands, attached to her gaunt body, always seemed to stand alone, foreign to her. The backs of her palms, strangely long and elegant, knuckles like polished, bone-beads at the beginning of each slim section of her fingers. Such hands at work patching-up torn cloth startled her.

How Ying Mei's mother had taught her early on basic stitches needed for day-to-day mending. Mending, or cleaning for others, was likely to be this unattractive daughter's fate. So Ying Mei speedily learnt to complete elementary sewing, carefully. Her fingers never lagged.

But despite her manual skills with needle and thread, the young, married woman's down-to-earth ambitions looked further into the future. A knack for business and bargaining must reap reward. Extending her husband's market had been her first aim. Selling thread barely fed the two of them. Let alone any children that must sooner or later come along.

Scratching together remnants of fabric, allowing nothing to go to waste, Grandmother Ying Mei could still remember all those years ago, starting work on small embroidered objects.

How she covered scent-bags, completed decorative hanging pouches and made fan cases with precisely embroidered insects, fruit, birds, animals and flowers. Doing his wife's bidding, Chang took these items with him when he went out hawking his wares. The quality of embroidery on the small items for sale was soon noticed. His business began to flourish.

Where previously he had been paid little attention as a simple hawker of thread, Chang was now sought out for the fancywork in his possession. From plain hawker, he became a renowned bag-pedlar. Women of fashion sent servants, requested private viewings of his wares. Ying Mei was soon employed in embellishing specific orders, exquisitely decorated pieces to be worn around the bodies of women from wealthy families. Slowly but surely, the married couple built up resources to set up their own small embroidery shop.

By then Ying Mei had borne two children, a daughter and a son. While Chang had been pleased his daughter was healthy, it was when Ying Mei presented him with a boy-child she saw the deepest love on his face; knew she had given him something of immeasurable value.

Chang and Ying Mei's firstborn was assisting in the making of goods by the time she was seven, learning her trade as she went along. The shop took orders, selling all sorts of embroideries. Grandmother Ying Mei continued to be, as ever, the source of advice, strength and motivation for her husband. Keeping a close eye on market demand, she fashioned things to be given as gifts, ornamental embroideries, items for practical use, theatrical costumes, collars, caps, shoes – she was a first-rate judge of what would attract a buyer. Business grew. A second daughter came along. A second son was born, then another. Chang nodded, was content.

Mei Si remembered. Grandmother Ying Mei told how she would pause from time to time, stretch and look around her, relishing joy in the silence. She felt the relief of one task ending before the next began. Was that passing instant, that moment of release, happiness she wondered?

The one thing Mei Si knew her Grandmother never did was put down her needle. Whatever her success in business, she believed her humble stitching skills were fundamental to her good fortune, her very being.

Mei Si dressed as a bride, waiting, remembered the aromatic plant bag embroidered with deer and cranes the old lady made and wore around her waist. Inside it, wrapped safe in silk, she always kept the tiny statue of Kuan Yin, Goddess of Mercy, given her by Chang's aunt. Taking out the statue to share her secret wishes, she looked at her stitches, appreciating the design, smelling the sweetness.

It was then, Grandmother Ying Mei said, she knew. Spring had come to every corner of her world.

Today, the tiny statue was in granddaughter Mei Si's hand - a gift.

"Rose Petals After A Storm", by Christine Johnson

Claire Evans sat, shoulders hunched forward and hands clenched, in the waiting room. She blinked under the stark lighting that cast dismal shadows below the eyes of those who, like her, came here seeking help. Their misery only added to the panic she felt mounting in her chest. The sharp smell of disinfectant invaded her nostrils. Every surface she looked at seemed inflexible, artificial. Uniformed staff bustled around her, their efficient steps fathoming the labyrinth of wide corridors. Claire wondered if the others sitting, waiting, felt like she did – invisible.

The memory came back to her how earlier that evening she'd stood at home, distracted, gazing out of the window. At some point thick clouds had rolled in. A lowering, oppressive sky promised rain to come. She imagined small droplets arriving to trickle down the glass, meandering along until they joined up together to grow larger and run faster, burgeon before fading; trickling away into nonexistence at the edges of the window frame.

She recalled how when she was a little girl she delighted in running into the garden after a shower of rain. Roses, she remembered roses. How she would shake a rosebush over her, pick up a fallen flower; feel herself melt into its petal-softness, sparkling and cool. But there was no running into the garden for her these days, no shaking and melting. Only a dull, persistent gnawing in her breast she couldn't resolve.

Pushing the picture of a looming downpour from her mind Claire had drawn the curtains; turned away as usual to seek the comfort of familiar things in her personal space.

Looking down, she'd placed one sheltering hand on her stomach. It was a gesture she knew by now, one growing more familiar as the weeks passed, time ticking inexorably on. But still her mind hesitated over what she knew was growing beneath her heartbeat; rational thought dilly-dallying, refusing to catch up with her instinctive deeper feelings, make a final choice.

It was in night's darkest hours, a time of shadows within shadows, that the clatter of heavy raindrops against the roof formed a brutal backdrop, drumming Claire back from dreams. An icy remoteness already gripped her when she awoke in bed, a weird chill that she felt raising goose bumps across her skin. It took a moment for her to focus on the piercing and improper pain, followed by the sudden, searing fear of it shooting through her body. The deep throb returned, insistent, for a second time, and then again and again, shaking her to her very core. She heard the desperate gasp shiver out.

'No. Please, please, no.'

But all lingering questions of clemency and choice seemed to dissolve with the awareness of a cloying wetness between her thighs, an unreal but building sense of an ill-timed ending, an absence that should not be there. Turning on the bedside lamp, Claire looked down. There it was, blooming; a spreading scarlet stain against her flower-patterned sheets.

Even so, she'd clung to hope, chosen to walk to get here, to this place of waiting. Shrugging into whatever clothes came to hand, leaving her hair a tousled mess she had forced her bare feet into shoes and set out. It was probably not the wisest thing to do. But walking, huddled under an umbrella, had at least provided her momentary escape; a sense of keeping going, not yet giving up. Placing one foot in front of the next, she pushed on with quick, nervous strides, trying to ignore the sickening, clumsy weight of the slowly saturating sanitary pad lodged against her body. Counting her paces, she silently implored them to walk her permanently away from dread, leave it behind.

'...eighteen, nineteen, twenty...'

She concentrated on the fat blobs of rain bucketing down, sucked out of the sky; until she saw with dismay how they splattered and exploded against the pavement, destroyed, before uniting to form what looked like unwanted, murky puddles. Rather than avoiding them, she strode forward, splashed on through. Counting turned to cursing.

'Shit, shit, shit.'

Arriving at last to sit inside, waiting, coldness from her damp feet climbed Claire's legs, allowed an ominous numbness to seep into her. She turned her head this way and that, found there were no clocks where she sat; nothing to measure the passing of time. During the journey to get here she'd clung to the slim chance that if she remained strong minded, unresponsive, everything happening around her might prove to be illusive, untrue. Surely, rain or shine, what she carried within could not have simply curled up and died? Now, going nowhere, she was forced to confront a totally new sense of time, dwindling, slipping away.

How could she have let things come to this, remained indifferent, so calm? She'd looked into things, weighed up her decision-making in terms of weeks: up to seven weeks for what was called medical, twenty weeks for surgical, termination. No need to rush. No need to commit one way or the other just yet. She was in control of a life changing beginning or a neat ending. That was what she had believed. Now her mouth was dry. Relentlessly, the cramps and aches kept building in her. She fought back, tried to ignore them.

There was no one else to share her situation. The other half of the equation responsible for the unexpected result on the plastic stick was well and truly gone from her life; the relationship over before Claire began to question the changes occurring inside her body.

Not that she had any regrets. A short-lived romance at best, one that neither party started intending to take any further, she'd seen him off at the airport. By light of day he seemed a virtual stranger. He'd even hesitated, checking his watch before moving closer for a farewell kiss. As soon as their lips touched they both stepped back.

'Be seeing you,' he said.

'See you,' she replied.

Despite the words, they both knew they would never meet again. He left. After, she felt no compunction about proceeding with her choice whatever it might be as one that was hers, and hers alone, to make.

What she hadn't realized, in the midst of all her prevarication and inner debate since, was just how far she'd travelled; how, unconsciously, she had started to create so many secret hopes and dreams around this new arrival. Instead of dismissing it, she understood at last this was something she wanted, embraced and possessed with a fierce joy. Rather than being something to destroy, everything in her cried out, told her that this was something she should have always known must prosper: something, unawares, that fulfilled a dream she had looked forward to all her life.

'Claire Evans?'

'Here!'

She followed the nurse along the corridor and into a tiny cubicle. They sat divided by a desk and procedure, the nurse opening a file and starting to take down details. Claire watched her, thinking the face matched the surroundings. It looked scrubbed; cold and marble-like in the light.

'You're next in line to see the doctor,' the nurse said without looking up. 'What seems to be the problem?'

Claire felt the savage wave of terror the blunt question carved through her. She squared her shoulders, fought against a rush of tears; a deluge welling up from within.

'I'm bleeding.'

The nurse paused. Her eyes flickered upwards.

'Bleeding, where?'

Claire gulped, tried not to choke on the words, tears starting to dribble down her cheeks.

'I'm…it's my baby.'

The nurse's questions that followed came and went in a blur, a drummed out patter, a well-organized gathering of detail leading to a short and snappy version of events so far. The interview ended.

'This way, the doctor will see you now.'

The next room Claire entered was small and characterless, inexpressive as the young man who occupied it. The nurse handed over the file to him and hovered, ready to assist.

Seated, caught between the two of them, Claire felt silence press down upon her. The doctor's quick examination revealed the immediate and damning crimson evidence of the sanitary pad, briskly disposed of by the nurse. Deadpan deeper probing by the doctor only opened further floodgates that made Claire wince. The contents of all spaces within her seemed to be draining away, to be left bleak and dry. At last it was over. The doctor indicated the nurse should see to the patient's needs; provide a fresh pad, enable her to staunch the inevitable further bleeding and assist her to dress once more. All this, communicated in silence.

By the time Claire took her chair his attention was elsewhere. He lifted the telephone.

'We'll send you for a scan, tomorrow, just to make sure.'

Her heart lurched.

'You mean there's a chance? The baby is still alive?'

His eyes avoided hers. She wanted to believe the slight tap of his finger on his desk was due to impatience at someone else, possibly someone not picking up fast enough at the other end of the line. When they did, his making of an appointment was swift, professional. Mid-process, he covered the mouthpiece, multi-tasking.

'Highly unlikely, I think. But the scan will confirm, either way.'

His words, emotionless and clinical, stabbed through her. Pierced, she swallowed, choked to the brink of crying as the doctor finished on the telephone. When he turned back to her she saw him respond to her collapsed features with a frown. She watched him correct the look, unknit the puckering of his brow, settling a well-rehearsed mask upon the surface of his face instead; a subtle study of kind heartedness, a trained tool he kept at the ready for such occasions.

'I'm sorry. A miscarriage in the early weeks, it's just - one of those things. Everything seems to be doing well but then... it's unfortunate, but not uncommon.'

Claire's hand reached up. It was a spontaneous gesture, a visual full stop that swept any further words from his mouth. Capturing them in her palm, she tightened her fingers around them.

Her mind whirled. 'Miscarriage,' what kind of word was that? It sounded like a vehicle bumping into something on a dark freeway going nowhere, smashing a wheel, leading to a breakdown. Perhaps hinted at some awful sort of blunder, a slip-up unable to be corrected? A humiliating debacle, Claire thought, that only descended further into one great big bloody washout and mess as far as he was concerned. And as for 'just one of those things' and 'unfortunate,' he may as well chortle and say it was the luck of the draw. No, she wanted to scream at him! There is nothing just or unfortunate about the loss of my child.

She scrambled to find her voice. Incapable of accepting hollow phrases that meant nothing to her, even less to him, she opened her mouth to describe the weight of her grief; how she recognised already the unbearable loneliness she would have to live with. Anger at his detachment drove her to search for phrases that would hook like barbs into his flesh, make him hurt as much as she hurt. But everything that came into her mind only travelled as far as her throat, tripping and stumbling over the unshed tears lodged there. Powerless, reduced, frozen in that silent moment, she reached out for support by clutching her stomach. But now she found it barren, nothing left within her but emptiness spaces. All hope withered away.

As she prepared to leave she thought she saw a brief ripple of relief cross the doctor's face. Thank goodness, it seemed to say, the worst bit is over. Despite all indications, this patient wasn't going to dissolve into a dramatic and showy, unpleasant emotional pool that would need attention before he could move on competently to the next, all-too-commonplace crisis. He turned around to his keyboard, improvised what was needed, busied himself printing out a form and handed it to her.

'For your scan,' he explained.

His tone farewelled her, he'd done his job well. Everything was fine, she understood it to say. Already his mind was moving on. A quick glance towards the nurse indicated he was ready for the next patient to come in.

Claire called in at Reception with the form, making the appointment that would confirm her baby was dead.

Stepping outside, she found the rain had stopped. A gentle breeze touched her cheek. As she watched, the early morning sun broke through and the sky lit up. The world seemed somehow sharper, washed clean, as if an unseen hand had reached out with a flourish and retraced the edges of everything. For one fleeting second it appeared sadness might roll off her, as raindrops rolled off rose petals after a storm, without leaving a trace.

Then reality flooded back. Everything felt strange, alien, as if she no longer belonged. She'd told nobody about her child. Now there was nothing to tell. Only absence filled the gutted space all around her. Later she knew she would need to find somewhere else - anywhere else to begin again, to start over. But for now, devastated, nursing only grief, she stumbled along; tracing a dry path   home.

"Humbling", by Dean Kerrison

The rooftop was reasonably bare when I returned at the end of the day. It was pleasant though. Surely the gods were appeasing me for an exhausting day, navigating the most congested city in the world, Istanbul. I walked to the ledge and looked out. To the left, the Blue Mosque flaunted itself in the background, perched above everything else. Just in case someone couldn't already see the mosque, its minarets – the six long, slender towers surrounding the multi-layered dome – were illuminated brighter than the salmon-coloured stream poured above and behind the mosque. A reference to the building as the 'Blue Mosque' to a Turk would be met with squinted eyes. It is the Sultan Ahmet Mosque. I wasn't sure how the 'Blue Mosque' caught on. It seemed simplistic, like calling Uluru the 'Red Rock'. Hagia Sophia wasn't so confronting. More like an old friend, it stood opposite me at eye level, just two blocks away. Its four minarets didn't shine with artificial light, only a faint glint from the waning sunset. The silhouette resembled an old, wounded man, who, done with the struggle, had shut his eyes.

I wasn't expecting my solitude to last. A nearly full sixteen-bed dorm was attached to the roof top, so someone normally appeared at that time of day. I was certain my German friend, Tomas, would join me to drink highly-taxed Efes Pilsen beer again. Or maybe he was Hans. Yes, Hans. Names got blurred on the road but my feet dragged their faces and stories like stones.

I looked back towards the door. Still no sign of Hans. A man sat on a white plastic chair against the wall in the shady corner, smoking a cigarette. Hair covered his face and he wore a dark beanie and a knitted sweater. I'd seen him in passing a couple of times in the two days I'd been there. He was one of the first guests in the dorm to rise and leave in the mornings – quiet and didn't make much of a fuss. He was never back by the time I'd go to sleep. His bed was always neat and he'd assumed a communal shelf for his food. He appeared comfortable, like he knew what he was doing – a disposition most travellers would normally only pretend.

He slowly tilted his head up and down, fixing his coal eyes on me while he exhaled smoke. I nodded back at him with a medium-rare smile, a bit more than a forced family photo smile but a little less than a finding-free-Wi-Fi-when-figuring-out-your-next-move type of smile. I turned back to Hagia Sophia.

'Where you from?' he demanded, resembling an immigration officer.

'Australia.' I moved a plastic chair and sat down, ready for the customary introductory questions. At that stage of travelling, I could carry out my half of the conversation with my ears covered, like a B-grade actor performing the same play a thousandth time, as long as the other person's neediness didn't start to kick in. Without any existing baggage, two people can detach their social masks and uncensor their words – there's no burden to be carried. So forget psychologists, I had thought, just send a troubled person to their nearest hostel. Someone would be willing to listen, especially if their worries were imposed on others. Back then I only listened because I was polite.

'What is your name?'

'Sam. And you?'

'My name Sajid, my friend.' He spoke slowly and deliberately.

'Nice to meet you, Sajid.'

'How old are you?'

'Twenty,' I said. 'How old are you?'

'I'm thirty.'

'Oh, okay.' We gazed around. I put my right leg up into a four-figure position. 'Where are you from, Sajid?'

'I'm from Syria.'

'Syria? I've never met anyone from Syria before.'

Sajid took another puff of his cigarette. He extended his arm to offer me a smoke but I wasn't interested.

'Is that a problem, Sam?' My shoulders and eyebrows compressed. Natural light had dimmed in the distance and many buildings were no longer discernible.

'European man just left quickly when I say that. You stay, yes?'

'Ah, sure.' I looked around to see if anyone was upstairs yet. 'What're you doing in Istanbul?'

'Sorry?'

'What are you doing in Istanbul?'

'I no understand.'

From what I'd gathered, his spoken English seemed satisfactory but this basic meet-and-greet was as far as our conversation could stretch. Maybe it was my accent. I went inside to grab the tablet from my bag. The only noise was the modest purr of devices charging at the wall. Others had returned downstairs though – their jovialities barked in contrast. Beer bottles gently clunked against each other and the ceramic tables. Hans' perfect English echoed through, probably trying to chat up the Scandinavian. She was pretty cute. Her thick blonde hair was always ponytailed but she had an overly long clown-like laugh. A concoction of oregano, paprika, cumin and other Middle Eastern spices flowed up the staircase. As I turned back outside, from over my shoulder I could see Sajid staring at me. He continued to stare despite my gaze. Breathing deeply through my chest, I loosened my shoulders. I sat down again and typed the question into a translate app, converting it to Arabic. I passed the tablet to Sajid. As he read, his mouth opened for a moment and he nodded.

'I come to Istanbul for three month,' he typed in Arabic and translated back to English.

'Do you have family here?' I typed.

'No, they are in Cairo. I will go to Cairo to meet them after three month in Istanbul. I have visa problem with Egypt.' He tossed his cigarette on the concrete and squashed it with his boot.

'Do you want to tell me what happened?' I asked with regret, checking my watch.

'I am not proud.'

I read this, backspaced it and handed the tablet back to Sajid without speaking. He stared at me without taking it. His knees and feet were touching their opposites as I leant further across, lifted my eyebrows and hit the tablet against Sajid's arm. He snatched it from me and began to type. Maybe Sajid thinks I'm annoying and he's going to tell me to fuck off, I hoped. Some Arabic swears would be useful for handling the scammers in the Moroccan souks, at least.

It was dark by this point. A cloud of bats soared across the sky to no apparent destination, safe in numbers. I heard the kettle brewing inside. A Japanese lady got up at five every morning, waking most of us to make her first of many cups of tea for the day.

I began reading Sajid's message. He sat still for the first couple of minutes, his body sloped over his knees, looking down.

'Because of the war Syria, we had to leave our hometown. The town was bombed and destroyed by the fighters and many people die there. I went to university and have civil engineering degree. I had great plan to help make Syria a glorious nation once more. My father had good business making pottery so he affords to pay for flight to Cairo with my mother and two brothers. They plead for me to come but there is a problem because my wife Rashida. She no have passport so I stay in Syria with her. We go south past the border of Syria and Jordan to the Za'atari refugee camp. I no have clue where many of my friends go. Some are dead definitely but others I will never find.'

The tablet slipped out of my sweaty hands into my lap. The last time I had to listen was just a bisexuality confession. I gripped the tablet on my second or third attempt and looked at Sajid. I wondered how I got myself into this. He adjusted his beanie and crossed his arms.

'Za'atari is very crowded. We line for hours to receive food and many people fight each other for small meal. It is very scary.'

Wow, I thought, poor guy! I squinted, scanning up and down the broken-English text. Sajid noticed and started fidgeting more, scratching his face, shuffling his feet. He leant back, reaching for another cigarette.

'Because of many health care difficulties I tell Rashida she cannot have a baby. We cannot give a baby the care he needs. And good life he deserves. But after some months she is pregnant. We fight but we no have the resources to have abortion. She wants to keep. So then I leave to beautiful Istanbul. I will not see Rashida again. I may have a son or Rashida is dead. It is very very difficult but if I stay we live in misery together. All the displaced people would do any things to have the way to leave possible I have. But I think I'm still a bad person.'

I didn't say anything. Hans was escaping work for two weeks. A pair of girls were evading America's legal drinking age. And me? I hadn't figured that out, which was okay. Marvelling at the ordinary somewhere foreign transcended waiting for the extraordinary to appear at home. At the time, I believed Sajid did the right thing – living in unhappiness was not an option. I was sure Rashida must've been okay, she must've had people around her who cared for her. I doubted Sajid would've left otherwise.

'*Allahu akbar* (God is the greatest),' cried the *muezzin*. The call to prayer came from the Sultan Ahmet Mosque, reaching us through a sound system. Like the nights before, no stars were visible and it was impossible to know if there were clouds. Air pollution obscured everything. The roof top light wasn't turned on either. The staff wouldn't do anything until they were asked. Sajid's arms were back on the chair arms again, right hand holding the almost-dead cigarette.

'*Ashhadu an la ilaha illa Allah* (I bear witness that there is no god but God).'

'You don't pray?' I said, half-bowing.

'No, not now,' said Sajid. He asked for the tablet again and started typing.

I was hungry. I wanted to go and find a waterfront stall selling *balik ekmek*, or fish bread as it was also displayed. A simple, tasty meal: fresh fish, lettuce, onion and tomato in long bread. And only half the cost of a pint.

'I have done wrong in this life. I no longer have opportunity to be granted salvation in the hereafter. Allah has taken my soul. He will punish me more in the next life and now I suffer while I wait. No amount of prayer can save me from this fate. I do not deserve His mercy.'

'*Hayya alal falah* (come to salvation).'

I could hear a bunch of people upstairs in the dorm now, laughing, making noise. Sounded like someone tripped over. The girl with the annoying laugh made no secret of her presence. I was cold, and my limbs were numbed despite my wishing to get away from Sajid. I wanted to give him a hug though, the type that says 'you've got the next one' like a soccer player consoling his teammate after an error. But this seasoned man was done with the struggle and like Hagia Sophia, had shut his eyes.

I still think about Sajid often. I wonder if he ever made it to Cairo. I imagine his family might have disowned him. He was once like the Sultan Ahmet Mosque, before civil war withered away his promise. I can't help but feel a splash of contempt for him now, which I feel guilty about.

Years after graduating from university, I moved interstate – away from my family – for the energy company I was working for. Ironic, considering the industry is a primary polluter of the skies, I've helped to damage the beauty that I deeply adore. During my absence, my dear ex-wife had an affair with her now-husband, a man my daughter calls 'Dad'. A doctor. He takes my daughter to piano classes and teaches her sports.

A man should only be away from his family if his interest is to better them. If they go down, you go down together; you don't abandon ship. Yet I found myself in a similar boat to Sajid. I have my doubts whether karma exists. Perhaps the universe sees things as black or white. It sees only my leaving my family, not measuring cause or intent – merely the action itself.

But how can you despair when there's the promise ahead of extraordinary things? Places that don't break up with you. You'll encounter people who see things differently – the ones who've experienced trauma. Such trauma lays a platform for their different understanding of life. They have strange ideas, unusual perceptions of reality, and seek alternative answers and outcomes.

I hope Rashida and her child are safe or at peace and nevertheless, I picture Sajid with his beanie off, kneeling in a crowded mosque, all facing the same direction.

"Stage Love", by Beverley Lello

Fantasy (noun) **2** an idea with no basis in reality.

I'm blinded by the lights so I can't see faces but I know they're out there, my parents. I'm wearing the costume of a Greek maiden mourning the death of her brother. I want my parents to be applauding me when the performance ends. I want them to join the crowd that mills around me afterwards saying things like: *Great performance. We're so proud of you. We'll tell all our friends to come.* And one of them will say, *And we have special news. We're getting back together.*

Realism (noun) **1** the practice of accepting a situation as it is and dealing with it accordingly.

'Can you come on the Friday? It's opening night.' I ask my mother first because I spend more time with her. We meet at the gym every Friday morning. Since the divorce my mother, Roz, has become obsessed with keeping fit. We start off on the walking machine. She sets a faster pace than me, with an incline, but I keep my pace slow and level. Running on the flat.

'I want to be in better shape the next time around,' she says. She's on the look out for a new man and has tried out several prospective partners, mostly acquired on internet dating sites. I steer the conversation back to my performance because I don't want to hear about her latest hook up.

'It's the best part I've had.'

'What's it about?'

'You've heard of Antigone, surely.'

'Of course, I just can't remember what it's about.'

'She was the daughter of Oedipus ...'

'The one who murdered his father and married his mother.'

'Yes, that one, but this is her story. Her uncle, Creon, wouldn't let her bury her brother who'd led an invasion against him. Antigone stood up to Creon and he had her killed.'

'It's very …'

'… sad? I don't like sad plays. Why can't you be in a comedy?'

A film of sweat smears my forehead and I'm forced to speak in wheezy puffs but Roz looks cool, breathing evenly. She must be at the gym more than once a week.

'I'm not a comic actor. I do tragedy best.'

'You always have, darling.'

I ignore this reference to something she obviously sees as a flaw in my personality.

'Are you coming, or not?'

'I suppose so. Can I bring someone? Will your father be there?'

They've been divorced for five years. They waited until my younger brother, Sam, finished Year 12. He used to say that living alone with them was like being in a cage with two hungry tigers and no other source of food. That's not how I remember it though. Tension? Yes, but all couples fight, don't they?

'I'm asking him and Cheryl to come on another night. It's on for two weeks.' I'd learnt that my attempts to manipulate them into getting back together always failed.

'I don't mind. I can be polite.' She increases her stride and pounds harder. 'Unless he brings that woman.'

'I'll get two tickets for Friday then.' I increase my pace, too, and our feet thump the imaginary footpath.

'So, what theatre is it in?'

'The upstairs one. In Richmond.' I can only gasp out the words now. I reduce the pace and slow to a walk. Roz keeps striding, a barely perceptible slick of sweat pasting her fringe to her brow. Her long red hair is secured in a high pony tail and it bounces jauntily in time to her pounding feet. I suspect she's put something on her profile about being keen on marathon running.

'Not that poky hole. I suppose we have to sit on milk crates with cushions on the top again. I had to do extra Pilates to get my back into shape after that last performance.' Roz also does Pilates and can perform quite a long monologue on the need to strengthen your inner core muscles.

'You don't have to come.'

'Yes, I do. I want to come. I love the theatre.'

Another quote from her profile, I suppose.

Roz slows the machine and faces me. 'It's not easy, you know. It's been five years.

I'm lonely. I don't want to be by myself and it's hard to meet people.'

I slow my pace to a standstill and we stand looking at each other.

'Roz continues, 'The internet dating is a gamble and I've had a few crazies – and boors. You know, I think a lot of men just want someone to talk at. My last one looked promising and I felt a flutter of hope but after ten minutes I was praying to be delivered from a monologue that badly needed editing.'

I don't know what to say. I realise she doesn't usually talk to me about her life. We move onto the exercise bikes, but not two together, so I practise my lines. *I spit on your happiness. You with your promise of a humdrum happiness – provided a person doesn't ask too much of life. I want everything of life, I do; and I want it now!*

I know this role was made for me. Not that my brother is dead and in need of burying – he was very much alive last weekend when we met up for a drink – but it's the stuff about humdrum happiness. I want more and because my parents have been at war for half my life, I've struggled to even achieve the humdrum.

My brother is content to compromise. 'Stop thinking they'll get back together. They hate each other, Charlotte. Accept it. Move on.' He keeps saying this hoping that repetition will batter me into acceptance, but I'm older than him. I have more memories of the good times: the camping trips, the time we went snorkelling at Ningaloo Reef, the trip to Fiji, the hiking trips in Tasmania, and the times they came to see me perform at Eisteddfods even though it must have been painfully boring to sit through all that reciting.

Then there was the Eisteddfod they didn't come – neither of them. I won three trophies that year because I was devastated, angry, hurt. I remember the adjudicator wrote: *An incredibly mature and moving performance from one so young. Excellent voice modulation and effective use of the restrained sob in the concluding line.* I'd been the spurned Queen Ann from Richard III that time.

I want to be sure that everything will be as beautiful as when I was a little girl. If not I want to die. Antigone had the right idea; she knew what made life worth living. I wondered if I could get my voice to produce a restrained sob when I say, I want to die.

'Talking to yourself again.' Roz is standing at my elbow, towelling and mopping. Her face is quite red now and I'm worried she might be overdoing it. 'I'm moving onto the weights,' she says.

'I'm learning my lines.'

'That's a relief. I thought you were contemplating suicide.'

'It's very intense. I'm hoping to impress.'

'Who?'

'The reviewer. Someone might be coming from The Age.'

'I'll exit stage left. Do some weights. See you in the shower.'

They've never taken my career ambitions seriously.

Rehearsals (noun) **1** a trial performance of a play or other work for later public performance.

I juggle my waitressing job in an Italian Restaurant in Lygon Street with rehearsals in Richmond. It's summer and hot and stuffy in the tiny cramped theatre but the play is fantastic and I'm humming every time I start rehearsing. One drawback is the director, Nadia, who's cranky and demanding. She thinks she's too good for our backstreet production and says things like, *You're not waiting on tables now, Charlotte. You can demonstrate a bit more passion.*

What does she know anyway? She has a job at a call centre telling people how they can save on their electricity bills. Most of us in the group are stuck in reality, being something we don't want to be. George, who plays Creon, is a solicitor and he says it's dull and deadly. He has money and I know some of it's been invested in the production; that's probably why he has the role and, even though he keeps forgetting his lines, Nadia doesn't lob him dollops of sarcasm.

Nick, the guy playing Haemon – my intended husband in the play – is still at university. At least he's doing what he wants to do. He's in the production as part of his masters and he has actually read the play in French. I try not to get distracted by wishing for the real thing when he says, *It's you I love and no-one else.* He's thin and when he embraces me I can feel he's all skeleton and hard bone. Do I feel too fleshy to him? I'm determined to start going to the gym three times a week because I know Antigone was thin and reed like but strong because she had to bury her brother alone.

Nadia's pretending to be a director again saying, *Save the bear hug for dress rehearsal, Nick.* Do I detect jealousy? Nick just grins and his lips are skin pink against the dark stubble on his chin and jaw. An appropriate look for a Greek prince.

Amateur (adjective) **1** non-professional **2** inept

Roz phones. 'I've bought my tickets. Laurence is really looking forward to it.'

Laurence! I can only think of Laurence Olivier but doubt whether someone that handsome would be forced to use an internet dating site. It's only a coincidence but later I notice my copy of Jean Anouilh's *Antigone* lists Laurence Olivier as the producer of a London production in 1949. Is this some sort of sign?

'That's nice,' I say. 'I hope he's not expecting the Melbourne Theatre Company.'

'No. It said on his profile that one of his interests is amateur theatre. I think he does some acting. That's one of the reasons I agreed to date him.'

Date. What era is she in? Still, I hang up feeling a bit happier. The last guy she brought along went to sleep and I could hear him snoring right through the second act of *Taming of the Shrew*. I haven't heard yet whether my father's bought his tickets. At least Roz didn't ask whether he was coming; she probably wants him to so she can show off Laurence.

Criticism (noun) **1** expression of disapproval; finding fault.

It's the night of the dress rehearsal and I think my performance has been good so far. Good, not great. I've hardly missed a line and when I did Nick rescued me. I think he knows the whole play by heart. He's actually been helping me learn my lines because he's only in the play for a bit at the start. I'm on stage almost the whole time and I've got some really long speeches.

At the end of the rehearsal Nadia really lashes out. It's her most impressive performance so far. George is told he was as wooden as a table leg and, as usual, I was told my passion failed to peak. Nick wins some praise though.

She says, 'Nice performance, Nick. You've got that mix of adoring Antigone and being puzzled by her intentions, just right. And Charlotte, you need to live up to his love.' Bitch. But then she adds, 'That scene when the guards drag you in, it's not just the guards holding you back.'

I might have to think about that.

Scrim (noun) **2** *Theatre* a piece of gauze cloth that appears opaque until lit from behind, used as a screen or backcloth.

Finally it's opening night. The performance is half way through and my big speech is coming up. The back of the stage is obscured by a scrim and this is how I enter. Two guards are holding my arms, the guards Nadia referred to in her dress rehearsal criticism, and I'm struggling to break free. The audience can't quite see what's going on and then the scrim lifts and I'm thrust forward by the guards.

Up to this point I haven't been able to get the audience distanced. I've seen Roz with her new man in the front row and felt the usual pang, *Why can't it be Dad?* Almost all the milk crates are occupied and that's a bonus because it's quite depressing performing to an almost empty theatre. But I'm not Antigone. I need to become the person who will give up the love of her life to do what she is sure is the right thing, bury her brother.

I think of the words of the chorus who introduced me at the start of the play. *That thin little creature ... will burst forth as the tense, sallow, wilful girl whose family would never take her seriously and who is about to rise up alone against Creon, her uncle, the King.*

And that's it. The scrim is no longer there. I stop thinking about the audience. I am Antigone arguing my right to bury my brother and the only person I'm focused on is Creon. I'm using all the passion I can conjure up to convince him that I had no choice. And Creon's sounding passionate too. He thinks he's right and his way is the best way and happiness has a different meaning for everyone.

Flourish (noun) **1** a bold or extravagant gesture or action

Then it's over. I'm dead. My lover, Haemon, is dead. We bow with a flourish and everyone in the audience is applauding and calling out. There must be at least thirty of them on their milk crates, and I think I see someone with a notebook and pencil and hope it's the reviewer from *The Age*. Even Nadia is beaming when she is encouraged out of the wings. She whispers, 'You broke free Charlotte. Great stuff.'

Rhubarb (noun) **2** noise made by a group of actors to give the impression of indistinct background conversation.

Later, in the foyer, we are absorbed into a rhubarb of conversation where people are lingering, mouthing unscripted lines and holding glasses of wine. Nick has taken possession of my hand. Roz is there with Laurence. He's a bit older than her with grey crinkly hair and a paunch which seems to suggest he's not a marathon runner. Roz glows when he says he loves the theatre and hopes he gets to see me on the stage again so he probably was telling the truth on his profile.

Epilogue (noun) **1** a section or speech at the end of a book or play serving as a comment on or conclusion to what has happened.

My father isn't here and I'm glad because that means he'll come with Cheryl on another night. Maybe by then my performance will be even better. I might even manage the sob.

Quotations are from Antigone by Jean Anouilh – Methuen Modern Classics 1958

"The Choices That We Make", by Judy Liu

The black circles under her eyes should have been proof enough that the situation at home had gotten worse, it had now become a case of pretending not to see and acting like you couldn't hear. "I might as well be blind and deaf," Alice Li thought to herself. Night-time was the worst as it was dead silent except that she could hear everything, from the thumping of her heart, to the ticking of the clock and she knew that on schedule the fighting would start. The walls seemed to close in on her and each spiteful exchange seemed to amplify all around her. Even after the fight was long over and both her parents were asleep her mind would still be wide awake with echoing sounds of their lingering exchanges both spiteful and hurtful that would haunt her for days.

Tripping on a stray rock on the pavement, the jolt had shaken her from her thoughts. It took more effort to walk to school these days, the combination of sweaty palms and shortness of breathe created a weak and fragile shadow of her former self. Anxiety was the root cause of all her problems, her sudden panic attacks had gotten worse as they became more frequent due to the lack of sleep and her unbalanced diet. Whenever one of her dizzy spells hit she needed to sit down and breathe heavily into a paper bag to control the amount of oxygen she was inhaling so that she wouldn't pass out. Each new day was getting more and more difficult, at night she would lose herself in her iPod and books in hopes that she could postpone the evitable sun rise signally another day she had not the courage to face.

School was a blur, her friends helped her in any way they could but she could see that each morning when she broke down and her walls collapsed that they could do nothing more but to watch as a small piece inside of her died. Her pain was like an infectious disease that she did not want to spread. Her grades were slipping but that was only due to her lack of sleep and how she had found it extremely hard to focus in class. Music class was the worst, her hands now trembled as she placed them on the ivory black and white keys, her heart pounding not with excitement or adrenalin but with paralyzing fear and anxiety. She had not been practicing, it was a secret that she kept. The piano at home was locked at home and she didn't have the key. She had begun to forget her pieces and made more and more mistakes, which was abundantly obvious during choir practice. Because of her mistakes everyone had to start from the top and she could her the whispers and the stares. Her music teacher finally asked her to take a break and even though she knew it was for the best, it still hurt that she was losing her role as the accompanist. In her other classes she would zone out, not fall asleep but get lost in her thoughts and the arguments that were said the previous night. It felt as if her mind had left her body and she couldn't control replaying the events in her head, the events that she wanted desperately to forget. Sometimes she would have no recollection of a class and relied heavily on her friends for notes and found herself struggling to keep up. She was beginning to feel completed disconnected with her friends, school and the world around her.

At home the tension was so unbearable that you could cut the air with a knife. No one spoke and even if something was said it was restricted to polite conversations and safe topics such as "How was school?" "How was work?" "Strange changes in the weather for this time of the year?" Communication had ceased within her house, everyone seemed to just go about their separate lives and the only link that was holding them together was the roof they shared over their heads. Sometimes she felt trapped and alone, being an only child did not help as she felt that there was no one that understood her pain. Yet on some level she felt happy, almost glad that she was an only child and that there would be no one else to bear this burden.

Alice looked around, her thoughts had overtaken her again. She found herself sitting on the steps at the front of her school waiting for her friend. She was early. Everything that she did these past couple of months felt robotic as if she had been switched to auto-pilot, her responses were routine and she felt that it was the only way she could prevent herself from getting hurt. If she didn't feel then she wouldn't fall apart. If she didn't fall apart then she wouldn't cry. She knew both her parents loved her but it was hard watching them tear each other apart. What they didn't realise was that every swipe that they took at each other was an indirect blow to her. After a while she realised that she needed to switch it off, otherwise the pain they were inflicting on each other would ultimately kill her. Yet everything changed during the last weekend and as a direct result she would finally be taking back some control. Unconsciously she rubbed her hands together and thought back to the events that had taken place the day before and when it finally occurred to her that she needed help.

Weekends were the absolute worst, at home there was no escaping the 48 hours that they would have to spend under the same roof. Alice didn't think that it had gotten this bad but this was largely self-denial. There used to be good times when things felt like they were back to how they use to be but these good periods seemed to get shorter and shorter. Before the mood at home was like a roller coaster, sometimes high sometimes low, but now there were rarely any highs. If the atmosphere was calm and there were no raised voices or the sound of shattering plates it was a good day. However this weekend started off bad as her Dad had come home in a lousy mood on Friday and it only got worse. Alice couldn't even remember what had set it off, usually dinner would be just her and Mum, Dad worked longer hours probably just to avoid confrontations but it seemed that even with the reduced hours he did spend at home there was always a reason for him to start yelling. She felt like she had to tread carefully around certain subjects and for some reason it seemed that she always managed to say the wrong thing.

It was a topic that she shouldn't have brought up, Music, she knew that whenever it was mentioned it would always upset him as well as her mum, but she had become tired by the excuses they gave her. She was sixteen and no matter how many times her dad said she was too young, too Australian or too naive to understand she sometimes just wanted to be heard. Piano lessons, Alice wanted to desperately wanted to play again and she needed her music teacher, who was both a mentor and friend. Her private music lessons had stopped a couple months ago when her last report card came out, according to her Dad her academic grades were more important and until they improved music was put on hold. No more practicing, no more playing, this was an extra-curricular activity and could only be resumed after she was back up to being a straight A student.

Yes a couple of years ago she would have let it go but she felt a surge of emotions that broke through her walls and everything that she had bottled up inside had just exploded. Her feelings, her thoughts and her opinions, did they not matter? Was she not allowed to make decisions regarding her life? Why is it that her Dad always thought he knew what was best? Was she not a member of this family as well and entitled to speak up? There were a lot of unresolved issues that had been buried over the years and finally she felt like they needed to be addressed once and for all. But what she realised was that there was no compromise, her Dad didn't understand and talking to him was like talking to a marble statue. Her feelings, thoughts and opinions did not matter after all and after such a confrontation one thing became crystal clear, anyone who lived under his roof had to follow his rules. Her Dad left the house after the fight to clear his head, and for once Alice went to her room and let go. She usually tried to keep her emotions in check at home but this time she had had enough. She locked her door and pounded her hands on the walls until they turned numb. She was frustrated, hurt and angry and wanted to everything to just stop. Her eyes darted frantically across the room and suddenly spotted her craft knife lying on her desk, before she knew it she had the knife in her hand. It was only when she hear her mom crying outside that she realised what she was about to do. Bursting into tears she dropped the knife and let her tears consume her, it was like a release, the valve had opened and she needed to express exactly what she felt on the inside. It had been building up for so long that as the tears poured out of her so did her pain.

As the hours went by she calmed down, sitting at her desk she thought about her situation. How long was this downward spiral supposed to last? Was it really worth it? Feeling returned to her hands and as her anger subsided all that was left was the throbbing pain and redness that she inflicted on herself. It was at this moment Alice realised that her emotional pain had become a physical one. As she looked out the window at the night sky something caught her eye, her year advisor had given it to her just last week, a flyer. Apparently her behaviour had caught the attention of one of her teachers and a special meeting had taken place between her and Mrs Verela. The flyer was for counseling and it read, "Need someone to talk to? Can't sort out your emotions? Help is available." Taking a deep breath she knew that it would be hard but this was her life and she had to make a change. She reached for her phone as she dialed the number of her best friend. She was going to make that appointment, it was time to stop living in the darkness that plagued her mind and walk towards the light. She wanted to smile again, to laugh with her friends, she was tired of turning it off and not feeling, it was time for a change.

Alice looked up someone was calling her name. Caroline had arrived, she was smiling an encouraging smile. This was something all her friends had wanted for her for a long time, to ask for help. As she stood up slowly her heart still racing, she could hear

Caroline say, "It will be okay, take my hand and we'll go together."
Turning around Alice took a deep breath, despite her situation at
home, the fights that will be forever embedded into her mind and
the painful scars that may never heal, she was determined walk out
of the shadow. This was her life and no one else's, her choices,
thoughts and opinions mattered and even though life was hard now
she had to believe that one day things would be different and it was
going   to   get   better.

"Iggy Poop", by Casey Millikin

Iggy Pop has just taken a shit on my kitchen floor.

If you didn't know that Iggy is a French bulldog—purchased in the vicious throes of grief—you might be assuming that I was enjoying the sort of evening that David Bowie had in 1978.

Unfortunately not.

My night involves staring at a brick of shit-smeared slate in Hollowditch: an end-of-the-line, lower-middle class suburb just down from Frampton (*The single mothers and their ADD spawn welcome you to Frampton!*) and smack-bang in the middle of country Queensland's Southern Cross heartland. Two months ago I packed my life into a teeny Toyota and moved here from the city. And I miss the city. Every day. It has become my twitching phantom limb. Anyway, tonight it's freezing. Big fucking surprise, it's always freezing in Hollowditch. It's hailing as well—you know, just to add to the misery of the whole affair—and the pucks of ice make gentle plinks as they hit my window. It'd all be quite soothing if I wasn't standing in the kitchen, examining excrement with a incontinent bulldog—who looks proud yet apprehensive—at my side.

I smooth the frown-line between my brows with two fingers as Iggy repositions himself to sit on the toe of my faded pink Ugg boot, which still smells vaguely of coconut oil after the Great Baking Mishap of last month: the afternoon a tray of handicapped Paleo muffins were unceremoniously thrown out the window, only to be replaced by a rescue dog.

"Why call him a rescue, anyway?" my brother had pontificated via Skype as I fussed over my four-legged distraction. "It's not like he was saved from the frozen tundra."

"He's a bulldog, Alistair," I said, pouring a large measure of cask wine into a chipped yellow coffee cup. "Not a husky. Bulldogs don't live in the frozen tundra. Anyway, rescue or not, isn't he adorable?"

Alistair leaned in for a closer look, peering through my computer screen with owlish eyes partially hidden behind round, thick framed glasses. "I think he's crapping on your floor."

Forty faecal-strewn days later, he was still evacuating his bowels on the same spot, I was still rubbish at baking, and Alistair was still chiding me for "running away from my problems". The more things change, and so it goes. Or whatever that saying is.

I roll out a handful of paper towel, sighing inwardly. *If I'm running away from my problems,* I think as I gently prise the turd from the floor. *The place I'm heading to is only serving to shit all over me—metaphorically and literally.*

I glance at the dog. "I should rename you Iggy Poop."

He sneezes.

"Good comeback."

The floor clean, I perch behind my computer, a glass of wine roughly the size of my cranium already waiting on the desk. This has become my nightly ritual: cheap shiraz coupled with a spell of cyber spying. A worn blue blanket wraps around my legs, and I remove and throw one coconut Ugg at a time across the room, tucking my stockinged feet snugly beneath me. Iggy perches on the hem of the blanket, chuffing softly.

"What?"

Brown eyes beneath a furry, wrinkled forehead rise to meet mine. He head-butts my leg softly, and then walks over to the fridge, his muscular rear settling before the door.

"You want food? You can't be fucking hungry."

He turns in a tight circle and sits again, gazing at me over his shoulder.

"I'm not feeding you. My kitchen tiles can't handle much more bleach."

The thought intrudes before I have a chance to stop it: *Mum, lying on the floor, unconscious. The chemical tang of bleach from the incessant floor scrubbing still sharp in the air. My knee socks were bunched around my ankles as I squatted down in my little private school pinafore, rolling her over, terrified at the trail of blood that had escaped her nose—*

Back in the kitchen, Iggy barks louder. I jump, my reverie broken. "No."

For a beat he simply stares. I try not to break eye contact—I've watched Cesar Milan's show, this is just a canine pissing contest. So to speak. We glare at each other for an eon before Iggy lazily raises to half-drag his backside across the floor, finally coming to rest at my feet. There is a strangled wheeze, a pause, and eventually a petite pop. Noxious odour floods my nostrils.

I cough involuntarily. "What the hell is wrong with you?"

He barks.

My patience thins and I yell, "Are you fucking retarded?"

A low grumble escapes him and he grasps the edge of the blanket, tugging it from my lap. I catch it.

"Iggy, no!"

He growls, gripping the only warm thing that I own in his saliva encrusted flews.

Now I'm growling as well. "Give me my fucking blanket."

So, it's Saturday night in shitty, shitty Hollowditch and I'm in my flat, half-stung, sliding across polished floorboards in socks, engaging in a non-consensual game of tug-of-war with a misanthropic, flatulent bulldog. I know—we all want my life. I pinch myself every day.

"Iggy Pop!" I bellow as he bravely and determinately drags me closer to fridge. "Drop it now or I will neuter you and hang your testicles from my rearview mirror."

His knobbly head shakes vigorously from side to side, jaws still fervently clamped.

"Iggy, I'm not playing with you."

He tugs violently. Thoroughly fed up, I let go. He falls heavily to his backside, the blanket shrouding his face. One insolent eye glares at me beneath blue poly blend. I gather him and the blanket up, carry the protesting bundle to the bathroom, dump it on the floor, and shut the door behind me. A lock on the door would be nice—one of those old fashioned keyhole ones—so I could crisply turn the key and gain even more satisfaction.

The door thumps as he head-butts it.

"Enjoy your evening in there."

He barks once, as if to say, 'Bitch.'

I kick the door lightly in response. "Mongrel."

Back at the chair, my arms cross my chest tightly as I try to ignore the subzero temperature of the flat. I drain my remaining wine in a large, warming gulp as the blue and white log-in page of Facebook glows from the computer screen.

Thump.

"Stop it, Iggy."

The keyboard clacks irregularly; the little buttons spelling out my email, then the convoluted string of characters that comprise my password. Hitting enter, I rise to refill my wine. To my left, the bathroom door periodically shudders.

"Iggy, you're either going to concuss or exhaust yourself. One way or another, you'll stop and I'll win." My butt settles on the seat again. "I'll always win. I'm bigger and you don't have conscious thought."

The wine sloshes as I put the glass back down on the desk. Facebook has loaded, and I'm scrolling through my friends list, looking for Gretchen, the pretty woman with the ugly name— *Gretchen*: it sounds like a side effect of food poisoning—absently tracing a finger across the rim of my wine glass as I go.

Thud.

And I can't find her. Between Gerry-the-stoner-that-I-dated-at-uni and Harry-the-janitor-from-the-pub, a gaping hole has been left. Gretchen has deleted me. *That man-thieving bitch.*

Thump.

I take another swig of wine, entering her name clumsily in the search bar, scrolling again, finally upgrading 'deleted' to 'blocked'. My smile is wan. In the background, the dog is barking. Loudly. Indignantly. The thumping resumes and the computer begins to ding softly—Alistair's weekly Skype call. Thumping, barking, drinking and stalking—it's all happening in Hollowditch tonight. I ignore the noise, wiping the side of the wine glass thoughtfully, thinking about relationship etiquette in the era of social media. Time ago, getting wasted and telling someone that they look like 'a malnourished bridge troll' would probably lead to little more than a tantrum and a huffy exit. Post the same thing on someone's Facebook wall and all of a sudden you're a 21st Century Hitler. A social media pariah. Thank god I blacked out before I could post the 'elephantiasis of the vagina' comment.

Thud.

A message from Alistair pops up beside the glaring void that Gretchen's truancy has created. 'Need to talk 2 u. Skype me pls xx'

My head drops to my hands. I miss the shit out of my brother. And it's all Gretchen's fault. This whole seething, pernicious quagmire. If she had of just kept her dimpled knees together...

Thud. Crash.

Unable to stand it any longer, I huff and rise to check on my four-legged scallywag. The bathroom is now a war zone of piss, poly blend and shredded toilet paper; Iggy glaring insolently from the battle lines, resting atop of a shower curtain that is now partially wrenched from its rail, the remaining unbroken hooks clinging precariously to the bar like passengers on the Titanic. I check the other side of the door and find a brand-new, bulldog-sized dent. I glance from the door to the dog. He sits placidly, staring at me through moist brown eyes—a furry Dalai Lama.

"You're going to pay for that."

He whines. Farts. Whines again.

I rub my forehead in frustration. "I actively fucking hate you; you know that, right?"

Woof.

"Yeah, yeah, and you hate me. Maybe one day we'll wind up as Turner and Hooch."

My phone begins to ring. Leaving the door ajar so that my miscreant can follow me, I pad over to the kitchen bench and glance at the screen. Alistair. I swipe my thumb left and hold the phone up to my ear. "Now's not really a good time, Ali."

Iggy begins to bark, obviously put out by the lack of attention he's receiving. As I twist to shush him, my elbow snags the bottle of shiraz. My mouth contorts into a silent 'shit!' as I reach to catch the bottle, miss spectacularly, and watch it land on the floor with a shattering crash. I curse, stare at the mess for five seconds, and curse again. I should have stuck with cask wine.

Iggy runs over and, with my battered iPhone wedged between my ear and shoulder, I bend to gingerly pick up pieces of broken glass with one hand, keep a slavering, possibly alcoholic bulldog away from the puddle of wine with the other, and wince as my brother chastises me.

"Jackie, what on earth is going on down there?"

"Oh, I'm just," I straighten to dump the shards of glass in the sink. "Apparently living in Baghdad at the moment."

Iggy barks. I point at him, giving an agitated warning that's ignored as he directs his attention back to the wine. To Alistair I say, "Let me put you on speaker."

"Are you at home?" Alistair's voice is magically magnified on the last two words as I tap the speaker icon, dropping the phone clumsily on the counter in the process.

"Uh-huh," I look around the kitchen, trying to remember where I put the dustpan. At my feet, Iggy is still carefully licking up spilt wine. "Hold on, I've gotta lock the dog in the bathroom again."

Iggy glances up in horror and scampers from the room.

"What do you mean 'again'?" Alistair demands. "What're you doing to that poor dog?"

Through the open door of my bedroom, I spy Iggy trying to wedge himself under the bed, looking a bit like Winnie the Pooh in the process.

"I swear he understands English."

"Jackie, I've got to tell you something."

The dustpan is on top of the fridge. I reach onto tip-toes. "Kinda busy at the moment," I grab hold of the handle and stare at it blankly. No brush. *Where the fuck did I leave the brush?* I search the kitchen. "Can you call back when I'm *not* falling apart?"

"They found mum."

My fingers twitch. The dustpan clatters to the floor. Despite the torrential storm still caterwauling outside, the kitchen seems eerily quiet.

"Jack?"

I lick parched lips and swallow. "She's okay though, right?"

Alistair's pause is just long enough to answer. My legs buckle and I sink to the slate, my eyes losing focus. My breath is shallow. The tap above my head drips. A pinkie toe is protruding from a hole in my socks that I'd never noticed before. Alistair is still talking. Saying something soothing, no doubt. The spilled wine remains stubbornly in my peripheral vision. *A drink, that'll help*, I think. *Warm, liquid anaesthesia.* But I can't make it across the room to the computer desk. There's no way my newly-motherless legs are going to prop me up. I'm half an orphan now. I gaze at the remnants of the smashed wine on the floor. Can I crawl over broken glass to have a drink? Is that classed as 'inappropriate behaviour'? What if you've just discovered that your nutty mother has finally found the courage to cap herself? Does that make it acceptable? Or can I just slurp it from the tiles like Iggy? Just how much can grief excuse?

Alistair is still talking. "I'm so sorry to tell you over the phone, honey. I really am. But at least you can stop looking for her. She never made it to Queensland, you know. They found her in a motel just by—"

"Shut up!" The shriek is ejected from me, a sound that has been lying dormant in my chest for some time, growing silently and malignantly; the tumour I've been carting around for months. It's pressed against my heart every night as I lay down to sleep. I've tried to dislodge it with litres of booze, hundreds of kilometres, and a dog. Nothing has worked. And now it's just burst through my centre like Sigourney's alien, and the wail that accompanies it—the sound that seems to be coming out of my own mouth—is one of pure, unadulterated, 90-proof sorrow. I take a ragged breath, half expecting to see a rotting hole in my chest.

Iggy stands at the door of the bedroom, bat ears pricked, head cocked to the side, watching me curiously.

Alistair is now pleading. "Come home. Dad misses you. And Gretchen's gone now."

My lip curls. *Gretchen.* That mutton-dressed-up-as-moll who sashayed over with her feathery flaxen bob and Katy Perry perfume to tear my family apart like Helen of Troy.

I need wine.

Grasping the side of the counter, I pull myself shakily to my feet. Iggy is still blinking silently at me.

"Jack? Are you there?"

I can picture Alistair removing the phone from his ear and frowning at the screen, wondering if the telephone towers servicing Hollowditch have decided to leave work early and go for a round of VBs with their tower-mates over in Wi-Fi. My knees are still unsteady and I wobble, scared to let go of the bench, not knowing if my lack of coordination is shock, booze or a combination of the two.

"Don't close down, Jackie-kins. Let me in."

When mum found out about the affair, she was tipped over the edge of a cliff that she'd been skirting for decades. Mum is—*was*—a bipolar OCD with a severe case of PTSD. She led a tumultuous life that was neatly punctuated by pills, psych wards and periodic, cry-for-help suicide attempts that were often foiled by her knee sock wearing daughter. When she busted dad fucking the wench, she disappeared, and said wench promptly moved in to take her place. I, unable to cope, unable to *flourish* in my environment, dropped out of uni and ran away. Like mother like daughter. Ostensibly, I went to look for her in the shitty, small town that she was born in: a hole in the land across the highway from Littlefield

(Littlefield: Slap your wife and shoot that Centrelink cheque up your arm!).

"I'm going to keep talking until you answer me."

I'm still on my feet, white knuckling the counter. Finger by finger, I release my grip, taking a tentative step towards the computer desk. The glass on the floor sticks into my socks. That hurts. I wince and pull my foot up reflexively, toppling over in the process. My elbow painfully cracks the counter. I've hit my funny bone. How ironic.

"I'll start singing soon. That'll get a response. You know how fucking horrible that sounds."

I sag back against the cupboard. My life has fallen apart, my family is splintered like worn wood veneer, and I'm so tired. And alone. Utterly, pathetically, completely alone. I've been fighting for months and, in this very instant, I'm finally done. I give up. It's all just too hard.

"*Mooooooooon river...*" Alistair croons.

Despite myself, I grin. Then a lone tear leaks out, rolling softly down my face. Its brothers quickly follow. And they feel good, you know? Cleansing. My head lulls back, eyes close, and I surrender to my sorrow.

But there's something scratchy on my cheek.

I open an eye, face scrunched against a sandpaper tongue, to see Iggy—my adorable, flatulent Iggy—sitting at my feet, earnestly licking the tears away. I'd been so entrenched in my calamity that I hadn't noticed him furtively making his way across the room towards me, but here he is. My furry support bra. Right when I need him most.

He barks. Studies me. Licks. Barks again.

Or maybe it's just that I was never alone at all.

On the phone, Alistair is still warbling, "*My Huckleberry friend...something...something...I don't know,*" his voice raises half an octave, "*the lyrics!*"

Iggy's attention slips to the counter and he lets out a guttural howl, matching Alistair's vibrato E note in a fingernail chalkboard harmony.

And I'm still crying, but there's something else growing in my chest. Something small and warm. "Oh, Hooch," I grab his furry face, "You delightful little shit." He twists from my grasp and makes his way over to the fridge, glancing at me expectantly. I smile.

"Ali?" I begin tentatively, "we're coming home."

"Glow", by C H Pearce

It's not such a bad crash, but the officer is worried that she's not talking. Pana thinks she's doing rather well. She stayed in her seat and kept very quiet through the whole thing, and didn't even scream when all the grown-ups did.

The airstrip is dark, lit by floodlights and the coloured flashes from moving vehicles. The officer in the crumpled suit is making arrangements to *contact the witness' parents, arrange an interview, it's a strange country, six to eight years old I'd say, it's got to be formal, do it once and do it right, hospital, it depends on the assessment, what an absolute cock-up, I'm sorry sir.* His mobile phone is pinned between titled head and shoulder: he speaks loudly into it and turns away, as though that would prevent her from hearing every rasping word, if not troubling to comprehend it.

People are being carried out of the plane on stretchers, down the side stairs, one, two, three. They are bloodied but seem to be moving with each step of the bearers. She isn't sure if they are just being jolted or if they are still alive. Behind them, a woman is walking slowly on the arm of another, with something pressed to a bloodied head. Her hair is matted.

The officer steps in front of Pana so she can't see. His suit crumples audibly when he crouches down. He fills the whole of her vision. He's got red and black stuff on his nice collar.

"There you go," he says evenly. "I told you on the plane that it was going to be alright."

The night air is chilly and Pana rubs her arms together. Her bangles jingle and it all feels stupid and pointless out here. She's miserable and cold. She runs her hand through her hair, and it comes away sticky.

"You very brave back there," he observes. That confirms it. Pana thought she probably must have been.

"I know you're a brave girl. Can you tell me your name?"

They retreat to the warmth of the airport lounge. Pana has a blanket wrapped around her shoulders, too, and her unreasonable body is still shivering. The pair walk small in the clean, quiet space. It is nearly empty except for the occasional frantic movement in the corners of her vision. Through glass windows so tall they reach all the way up to the ceiling, they have a view of the airstrip. She hovers a hand over the glass, and can feel the cold air creep towards her, and the blast from the overhead heating pushing it back.

She's watched all the passengers and the flight crew being carried out lying down, or being spoken to and having their details taken before they're allowed to go. Pana wonders when she will be allowed that, too, and where she would go.

The officer is still on his phone. Now it's to someone else. He holds one wrist limply, close to his chest, but he must be okay, because she saw him wave away the ambulance officer. When he thinks no one is looking, he also manages to light up a cigarette, wincing, and then another after he drops the first with fumbling fingers and grinds it into nothing under his heel. It squeaks angrily on the airport floor.

"It's fine," he says.

Pana looks away, too. This time she presses her hand against the window and stares through the gaps between her fingers. It's icy to the touch and already they're starting to go numb. The airstrip below is filled with little coloured lights in darkness. Some are moving: other stop for a moment, then resume. One orange light doesn't move, and appears bigger than the others. Pana wonders if it's a fire. Perhaps it's been put out and she's just seeing it all wrong. Perhaps she imagined it and there never was a fire at all.

She knows the lights all along the cabin went out, and when they came on she saw whole panels coming down from the ceiling.

There were noises in the undercarriage. Horrible noises, like an animal's cries, but no animal she's ever heard of, or thinks should be allowed in any zoo. There was a man, no, a something. A something that scuttled across the ceiling, dripping darkness, and underneath...

She can't think about that. Pana wonders how long they'll have to wait before her mother and father come and get her.

Her fingers have gone numb. She snatches her hand away from the window and tries to rub it back into life with the other. Anyway, it must be wrong. It wasn't one bit like an aeroplane crash on TV.

Pana begins to listen searchingly for something to twist and untwist and make sense of it for her, and then present it neatly back. *There was some superficial damage in the course of, yes sir, most notably to the cabin lights, all of them, yes sir, I know sir,* the officer is saying into the phone, *before I got the situation under some semblance of control.* Pana likes the words the officer uses on the phone, although it sounds funny and slow, like he's trying not to swear. It almost sounds like her mother and father speaking to each other, but not to her. And it does begin to make sense of what she remembers.

She wants to tug at the officer's sleeve and *say I need a bath, I want to be put to bed and told there are no monsters, and I want my mummy and daddy,* but she is, after all, nearly eight, and she's no longer sure about the monsters.

Instead, she makes her mouth its darkest frown and tells the window, severely: "My Gran is coming to pick me up."

Finally the officer stops talking and pays attention to her again. She can see him approaching in the reflection, and turns around. He seems pleased, and crouches down close.

"Good girl," he tells her, and then he's gone again, up and away, back to the phone. "It's alright. She just spoke. I think I should still take her in, all the same." The phone says something back, apparently, because he says *right you are, sir* and hangs up.

"Can you tell me your name? My name's Wilfred."

Pana thinks this is funny because he is clearly holding a piece of paper with all her details on it. It's facing towards her, crumpled sideways inside a clear plastic bag: it says KALPANA in big letters at the top, and her surname and her destination and contact details for home and her parents and Gran, who is coming for her presently. She saw him get it from the flight attendant, her escort with the pretty fingernails who promised she would stay with Pana the whole time, before she herself was ushered away. It's got red and black stuff on it, too, but that's all sealed up inside the plastic.

"I know," says Pana miserably. "I heard everything. I saw something, too. I didn't mean to."

"Did you, Kalpana?" Wilfred says. "That's good. That's very good."

"My name is Pana. Only my parents call me Kalpana. Your name is Wilfred Walden. You were escorting a prisoner. I heard you talking and swearing a lot on the plane. Are you really a police officer? You're wearing a suit."

"You're a clever girl, aren't you, Pana?" says Wilfred Walden.

"I saw something," she repeats. Her mouth is dry.

"Young lady, I believe you. Now you believe me. It is all taken care of. We just talked, and now he's gone his own way. You're safe. He won't be coming back."

"Your arm–"

"That's how we usually talk."

"You said you'd take care of it, and you did. I know you stopped him doing something worse. I know it. We landed alright because of you."

Walden smiles. It is distracted and mildly startled-looking, and tugs at his wrinkles. "And there I was thinking about everything I could have done better. I ignored multiple warning signs..."

He clears his throat and looks at his phone and pats his coat pockets. She can see the corners of more snap-locks peeking out.

"You don't have to say anything you don't want to, now. We'll do the interview later, when the others arrive," he says slowly, and she can tell he really wants to say something else and he's trying hard to say that instead, like the not-swearing. The words scratch up his throat and climb out slowly. He coughs again but it doesn't help. He needs to cut down, Mummy would say, in a voice so that Pana would know it was the truth.

"Says here you're an unaccompanied minor. We've got your parents' contact details. But Mummy and Daddy aren't picking up right now, because it's nighttime in Rome, see. They'll be sure to give me a call back in just a few hours. I'm going to take you to the hospital until then, for a checkup. They'll take great care of you, and your granny is going to meet you there and wait with you. And you'll get a few hours without some old bugger talking nonsense and asking questions when he shouldn't be."

Pana's hand shoots out and grips the officer's. She's surprised at her own strength – he can't wriggle out. She isn't letting go.

"Don't leave me until they come for me."

"My goodness. You're strong, too, as well as all those other things, aren't you? Okay. We'll stick together, you and I. Just let me send one more message and we'll drive to the hospital."

Pana lets go. Walden's working the mobile phone with his free hand. She realises, awfully, it's the injured one she's been gripping.   He   doesn't   seem   to   notice.

"Torvald's Year", by C H Pearce

"Did I get it? Do I get my Year in Light? Have I suffered long enough? Have I suffered well?"

Torvald nearly tugged on his manager's shirtsleeve. That would have been the end of it.

All his family told him it would be wonderful if he were to take it up. The boy deserved it, they said. Torvald had laboured in darkness for many years. Every day he moved earth and ore through the long, winding tunnels in his barrow.

"It will be wonderful," they said.

"You deserve it, boy."

It must be true: he heard them clearly. They said they hoped his application would be accepted this year.

Torvald kept his head down respectfully, so that his manager could only see the dome of it. It was dark and bald and slightly shiny in the sickly glow of a lamp. On the top was a light fuzz, wispy pale, like mould on the skin of a peach. His hands were on his barrow.

His manager flicked through the forms. Torvald glanced up sadly, noting every passing page had a red stamp on it.

He hefted the weight of the barrow to ready it on the tracks winding up to the ore deposit. It felt comfortable and familiar on his callouses, which had moulded themselves to the barrow handles long ago.

"Accepted," his manager said. He did not look up.

Torvald's hands fell to his sides. They hung light and still in the close mineshaft air.

"That's wonderful," Torvald cried. He brought the hands forward to wring his manager's, then thought better of it. He paused with them halfway outstretched.

His manager agreed that it was wonderful, and told him to empty his barrow at the deposit on his way out. It was 15:48, he said, by his armplant.

"You're due to clock in *precisely one year*, Torvald. I can wire the date so you don't forget. At 15:49. There, I gave you an extra minute: now you must tell me what the Light is like."

He grasped Torvald's still outstretched wrist and wired him the date, with a counter. It burnt unpleasantly all the way from Torvald's armplant up to his optic nerve. He tried to keep the grip steady.

"Compatibility issues, or impulses to upgrade," his manager observed, clicking his tongue. This was no casual observation, as Torvald knew: it was digging. He wanted another compliment on his fresh-fitted purchase, which Torvald, in this instant feverishly well-disposed, gave him in spades.

"I *love* your armplant," he said. This was rather in excess of what served to pass the time at work. As he spoke Torvald cocked his head sharply and pulled up the message on his eyeplant screen. He had one Year in Light, one beautiful year upstairs ahead of him, and it was ticking down right in front of him. *Three-hundred-and-sixty-four days, twenty-three hours, fifty-seven minutes.* He tilted the head back and the image flew away.

His manager was silent. He coughed and cleared his throat and tried to draw himself up, and bumped his head on the mineshaft ceiling.

"I'm saving my Year in Light for retirement, of course," he pronounced loftily, rubbing his skull with his free hand. "What a good idea to do it early. While you're young and mobile and can properly enjoy it. I wouldn't have thought it of you, Torvald: you always keep your head down and have no initiative. Do tell me what it's like in the Light, when you get back."

His manager's course was the reasonable one, Torvald knew. He kept the armplant against his manager's with increasing awkwardness, and wondered if he should transform it into a handshake. The usual approach to one's allotted Year in Light was, naturally, to save it until Redundancy at end of life. Retirement, at the earliest. Everyone works better, does better, lives happier, with something to look forward to. Reckless people who used theirs up young always came back downstairs sad and quiet, having nothing more to look forward to again.

Torvald had observed this in action, but he had seen something else, something he privately thought worse. Worst of all was when people saved it and saved it and became Redundant and died before they could take it. This happened frequently. This was the thought that made him shiver: he couldn't stand it brushing against his brain for more than an instant. What if he grew too old to fill in his forms and hobble his way to the elevator leading up to the great open surface? What if he died, suddenly crushed in a minefall with his barrow and a load of passable ore, and never saw the Light?

"Thank you," said Torvald, and wrung his manager's hand, ignoring the sparks. He wheeled the barrow all the way up the tracks to the deposit, pushing it at a run.

As he ran he thought that people knew. Every minute he lingered downstairs was a minute less up. He was flying. They unstooped from their barrows and uncurled from their digging, and several of them clapped him on the back in passing. He emptied the barrow, clocked out, and ran all the way home.

Here, too, they congratulated him. They hugged him and shook his shoulders. They told him he deserved it, to enjoy it, he had worked so hard. How wonderful and how novel: good luck: he was very young, wasn't he?

Torvald felt he floated all the way upstairs. He took the elevator. He had a return pass, a single, with one way left for when the counter ran out. That was of course nearly a whole year away.

"How are you enjoying your Year, dear? How much longer to you have to go? My screen's not working," asked the armplant. It was Auntie: her tremulous voice crackled through it. Torvald held it close to his face.

"It's beautiful," said Torvald. "It's very beautiful. How is the mine?"

"Voice only. Screens aren't permitted," Uncle was saying. "You know that. Don't tell us too much, boy. Not to us poor shits who have never seen the Light. Do you want to spoil it for us?"

Auntie shushed him and shouted into the armplant, having decided to compensate for the lack of visuals with volume. Her weak voice quavered with the effort.

"The mine is good work, honest work. It all goes to support upstairs, so people like you can enjoy it, dear boy, in your Year. You are *very young* to be taking your indulgence now. We miss you here at work. I do not complain: I only say your family suffers and labours, as usual. Are you having fun up there? When are you going to come back to work?"

"In two-hundred-and-forty-six days, three hours, and five minutes," Torvald read out. He felt his throat tighten as if to crack in making the words, but the voice sounded out with an evenness foreign and distant.

The light shone on his face, warm and lovely all over him, and the wind was shifting the leaves in many tall and slender trees. His downstairs eyes, large and pale, still blinked in it. As he spoke he curled and doubled over upon himself with guilt as though he were again held within the mine. He spoke evenly.

Next his mother and his father came on the line and checked whether he was enjoying himself, too, while they suffered.

His crouch became a ball and he and whispered back that he *yes, he was enjoying himself, he was practicing reading without mouthing the words, he wanted to get through everything in the great library before his year ran out, and the sky here was so open you might fall off the edge of the world, and sun, the sun, the sun was beautiful.* He was so sorry not to be working and earning and suffering. He didn't know what to do with his hands. What a good time he was having, but was it alright?

His parents said they were glad and they would go back to suffering presently, which would occupy them for some years. One day when they were old and deserving, they might enjoy what he was enjoying too.

Torvald rocked himself back and forth.

Then he uncurled and lay on the grass for some time, blinking at the open sky. He put a book over his face.

When he was not quite halfway through his Year in Light, Torvald sat outside the library determinedly reading in the sun. He had learned not to mouth, nor to have his armplant read for him aloud.

He found the sun rolled off his skin and the wind sounded dry in the trees. He could think of nothing else but his family and his manager, suffering and labouring in the mines while he enjoyed the Light. Was it right? Was it proper? Was he a good boy, still, or did that slip away in the open air outside the mine?

He wrung his hands. They were growing soft and unfamiliar.

Torvald cut the year in two.

At one-hundred-and-eighty-two days, twelve hours, zero minutes, Torvald used his one-way ticket and took the elevator down.

He ran all the way back to the waiting embrace of his family. He rapped on the door and flung his arms out expectantly wide.

"What are you doing here?" said Auntie. She held the door open just a crack. It was dark inside, with the tellybox going, and he could smell stew cooking.

"I'm back," said Torvald. "I had to come back to help you in the mine. I couldn't enjoy the Year in Light while you suffered. I was silly and young and indulgent: I didn't deserve it. You were all right. I'm sorry."

Auntie creaked the door open wider. Uncle was shuffling over. He raised his balding head, and clasped Torvald's shirtfront, dragging him down very close, as if for an embrace. His weak eyes were bulbous and quivering.

"You're a fool," he whispered. "You gave it up?"

He began to laugh. It was hoarse and hacked up his throat like a bad cough.

"Come here! Come here, everyone! It's the young prodigy! He gave it up!"

"That's the funniest damn thing I've ever heard," said his mother and father. They were hunched over staring at the tellybox. They didn't get up. "Oh, well, you'd better come in and have some dinner, Torvald."

The next day Torvald rose, dressed, clocked in and took up his barrow, and wheeled his way down the tracks.

"You're early, Torvald," said his manager, checking the time on his armplant. "Six months and two minutes early. What happened?"

Torvald nodded, and said nothing. His great pale eyes quavered in the lamplight as if with some luminescence all their own. His manager remarked that Torvald's eyeplant was setting in with rot or leak, and still needed upgrading. It made his peach-fuzz skull look heavier on one side, and his cheek wet. Torvald imagined the white mould had caved in part of his head.

"You should get that seen to. I keep telling you that. I thought you might have listened by now."

His hands ran across the barrow handles, familiar and cool. They caught splinters, but this would pass. He hefted its weight and it tethered him down and he proceeded along the tracks deeper into darkness.

"Second-Hand Light", by Kat Pekin

"Ask me, Ava," Mum says. We've been watching the news about the meteor showers. The same thing is on all the channels. Because the news keeps talking about it, I really get into my drawing so I don't have to see. When I show Mum my dog drawing her eyebrows scrunch together in that way she does when she's angry.

"Do you want a dog?" she says. "Ask me for a dog."

I nod.

"No, use your words, Ava. Do you want a dog? Say 'yes'!"

I nod again and want to cry. *I don't say words, Mum.* I wish she'd understand. *You know I don't say words anymore.* Mum turns off the news and says we need to sleep.

Mum wakes me for school earlier than she normally does. She has to work, she says there's emergency at the hospital. I want her to take me with her but she says I'll be safe at school. While she makes me my Vegemite sandwich for lunch she says sorry for yelling, and maybe I can have a dog next year. She tries to trick me into saying something back sometimes. Mum's a really smart doctor, but sometimes she's a really silly mum.

"Walk right home, Ava," Mum says as I leave for school.

She watches me from our front door. My school is at the end of our street. I don't know why she watches me. Maybe she thinks I'll disappear too.

I love living on Mt. Coot-tha. From my treehouse I can see the whole city light up when it gets dark. During the day, I swear I can see the ocean way, way back in the distance.

There aren't a lot of kids at school today. Their parents kept them home, I guess. Some of the teachers are gone, too. When I go to eat lunch I hear some of the teachers talking in the office, they're saying stuff about the meteor showers and wondering if the other teachers have really disappeared. More here.

Dad and I had been watching the lights the night he went away. There was a really big bang. Like thunder. It was so bright I had to scrunch my eyes closed. When I opened them, Dad was gone. He wasn't the only one. The next day loads of people had gone from all over the place.

When I get home after school, I find a note Mum left me on the fridge.

Ava,
I'm taking a nap. Think of something you want for dinner, and do your homework! ☺

Love Mum

I smile. Mum leaves these notes so I won't feel like she's forgotten me. I don't. And I know to finish my homework. I'm ten, not a baby. When Mum's works hard days at the hospital, sometimes she rests in the afternoon and when she wakes up we order takeaway. That's how we always do things, Mum and me.

I keep my backpack on while I make myself a Vegemite and cheese sandwich then go out the back door to my treehouse. I climb the ladder one-handed so I don't drop my sandwich. The ladder has only five steps on it. I haven't fallen off in ages.

Dad made the treehouse for me when I was just five. He always said the tree was made to have a treehouse in it. He said it had flourishing arms. That made me laugh. "Trees don't have arms, Dad!" I told him.

I look around the treehouse at my bean bag and my drawings and my curtains I made myself from old tea towels. I wish I had a dog. Or a cat. Even a bird or fish, or a mouse or guinea pig. It would be nice to have someone with me in my treehouse while Mum takes a nap. I wonder how I could get a dog up into the tree with me. Maybe I can tie a rope to a box and lift it up that way. Dad would be good at making something like that.

I unzip my backpack to get out my homework. I take Dad's beanie from the little hook on the wall and pull it onto my head. It's my treehouse hat. I think Mum knows I have it, but it makes her sad to see Dad's things so I don't wear it in front of her. Mum asks me a lot if I'm okay in my treehouse. Dad disappeared out of it, so I think she thinks I might be scared of being in here alone. But I'm not scared. I just wish I'd kept my eyes open that night.

I do my maths homework first. It's easy, adding and taking away stuff. Then I do my spelling words and then I get to read. We're reading Matilda this term. It's about a girl who likes to read more than anything else in the whole world.

I sit in my blue beanbag and read and read and read. I'm only supposed to read one chapter but I keep going. My teacher won't know. It starts to get a bit dark but when I check my iPhone it's only four o'clock. Maybe there's a storm coming. I turn on my phone light.

I keep reading and I'm up to the part where Matilda's Dad doesn't believe she solved a tricky maths question in her head when my phone light goes out. Last I looked, the battery was at forty-six percent. Then out my treehouse window I see little lights. I love watching the city lights turn on, building by building. Mum bought me binoculars for Christmas so I can see better. I crouch by the window and look through my tea-towel curtains. It's cold tonight. I'm glad I have Dad's beanie.

The lights start up like normal. I watch the big blue building that looks like it has steps on its roof light up. Below that I can see speedy lights of cars sliding around the streets. But then everything goes black. Not just the buildings, the car lights too. Like someone's turned off the light switch to everything.

Then I see lights again. This time they're in the sky and they're falling from the edges of what looks like a huge box turned up on one corner. White lights also beam out the box's sides as it floats just above the top of the buildings. My eyes open wider than I've ever opened them before. It's a spaceship. I feel like there should be the kind of noises I hear at the airport when planes take off, but it's quiet. Maybe I've suddenly gone deaf, too.

A ramp comes down from the bottom of the spaceship. At first I think there's water pouring out. I grab my binoculars to see better. It's not water; a bunch of little creatures are falling out of the ship. I drop my binoculars, grip the sides of Dad's beanie and pull it down around my ears. I'm shivery but not from the cold.

The creatures must be speedy because after only a couple of seconds I see three little dark shapes hopping over our back fence. They're smaller than me and look like bald kids with heads three sizes too big for their bodies. They sure look strange, but they don't make me want to run away screaming. Maybe I'm too scared to be scared. If I had to rate their scariness from one to ten I'd give them a two. Their kooky eyes I give a three, which is generous since it's two more than they have. They each have just one big, glassy eye. They're almost cute, except that noise they're making.

Years ago, at the zoo with Dad, we'd been watching the tigers eat and one of them swallowed something wrong. It made a weird gargling sound, and then made a funny barking noise to try and cough up whatever was caught in its throat. Eventually it coughed it up and then it let out a high-pitched sneeze. That's what these creatures sound like, coughing and gargling and pitch-sneezing at each other.

One of them, he looks like a boy, bounces up onto our roof like he has springs in his feet. He lands silently and hops towards our chimney. He peers down and then makes that coughing noise to himself and disappears down the chimney like a weird little Santa.

The other two are at the front door. I can't decide if they're boys or girls. I watch one of them point at the door and it just opens. The critters disappear into my house. What are they looking for? Maybe they're lost.

I hear glass crashing inside my house and now I'm a little scared for Mum. What if they hurt her? I hope she's hiding like I am.

I hear a pitchy little sneeze and one critter bursts out of the chimney. He arcs through the air and lands back on the roof, then hops onto the ground beside his friends. He bounds up and down like an excited puppy. Maybe he's never seen a chimney before. Or maybe he had fun using it like a chute. I guess anything can be fun if you play with it. He seems happy. The chimney leads to the living room. Mum's napping on the couch in there.

The other two creatures make a cough-cough-sneeze sound at the roof-jumper and then suddenly flee to the fence the way they had come over. The roof-jumper squeals like a teakettle, but he stays behind.

Then he looks up. Right at me. He crouches like he's preparing to spring and then he flings himself into my tree. He hops from branch to branch like a possum and I scoot back into the corner of my treehouse. I pull Dad's beanie further down my forehead but I don't cover my eyes. I want to keep them open. I'm not scared.

The roof-jumper sails through my window and lands silently on his chubby webbed feet.

He looks surprised. I think. Hard to tell with that one weird eye. He doesn't come closer or make any noise. He cocks his head at me like a dog hearing a strange sound. I wish I had a real dog.

Maybe he's trying to read my mind. He looks at me sideways, the same way maybe I'm looking at him. He takes a teeny step closer to me.

He doesn't make a sound. Not even a little cough.

A flash of sheet lightning blankets the sky, and the wind picks up. The smell from the pine trees in our yard tickles my nose. I sneeze twice.

Then I hear his voice. "Ava?"

"Dad!" I cry. My voice works again. But this time I keep my eyes open. "Where have you been? I've got so much to tell you!"

"The Charity Shop", by Fiona Perry

There she was, long-dead Mary, my mother, staring back at me from my own reflection in the shop window. There was no mistaking the geography of that face; deep marionette lines, thin lips and circular alert eyes. It is funny how I see her most often in myself when I am about to do something that she would strongly disapprove of.

I was pretending to pay attention to the window display while calculating my next move. I stared at the two headless mannequins with their garish-coloured summer dresses and the stack of old faded blockbuster novels at their feet. To my mind this holiday-themed diorama had a faintly sinister air; the central feature was a hard, battered suitcase on top of which two pairs of wire rimmed spectacles and a pair of old fashioned ladies' T-bar shoes had been carefully arranged - in an effort to look vintage or shabby chic I expect- but oddly it reminded me of my mother's regular, empty threats to leave my father. The packed suitcase placed provocatively in the hall, always a prelude to them patching things up. These long forgotten recollections keep appearing now that I am home again. I badly needed a bit of distraction.

At last I saw a customer walk towards the counter. I could enter the shop now without being immediately noticed by *him*. I needed a little time to compose myself before I would feel ready for conversation. Also I didn't want to give the impression that I had come here solely with the intention of speaking to him. That was not the case. My belongings still hadn't arrived from Australia. I had a compulsion to buy books because I had started a project of re-reading the classics of my youth. It intrigues me how different an impression of a book can be when read for a second time nearer to the end of life than the beginning.

I positioned myself in a corner of the shop to read the spines of second hand books in the hope of finding Jane Eyre or Wuthering

Heights amongst the Jilly Coopers and Danielle Steeles. I struck gold with student copies of Madam Bovary and a book on Zen Buddhism; one that I fondly remembered reading during my hippy phase in the 1960s. I occupied myself for a few moments conspicuously reading the blurbs.

Despite the proudly displayed new shiny Fairtrade stock, I always think that these places smell of old handbags and their contents; unlit matches, greasy rosary beads and compact powder. A leathery, sweet, musty fragrance- the distinct, intimate scent imparted by discarded objects. *Listen to me, getting all poetic and pretentious.* "If there is one thing a girl doesn't need it is an education" I could hear Mary, "you should get your nose out of that book, men are frightened of clever girls".

I wandered over to the counter to pay. I handed him the books and asked, "You are here again today, you volunteer two days a week?"

"I do indeed, Tuesday and Friday. Sure it keeps me off the streets", he said and laughed, revealing a decent set of teeth, every one of which appeared to be his own. "In a former life I was a manager in retail. Just these two books?" he asked.

"Yes. I am just back from Australia where I lived for a long time and I am re-reading old books, keeping myself busy. I am Anne by the way."

"I'm Peter. Australia? What on earth brought you back here? *In the winter?*" and he smiled again and I noticed his hands; big and manly but with extremely clean finger nails, resting on the books. He was wearing a wedding ring.

"Oh, we all come back in the end. I am not a hot weather person these days. I missed Ireland. The extended family here". Lies. My stock response to strangers who ask why I have come home.

"What did you do out there?"

"Nursing. They were desperate for nurses in the 1960s when I left for Australia." At least that was the truth.

"Is that so?" he said handing me my change. "Listen, if you find yourself bored and you enjoy having a rifle through second hand things you should get yourself to Greyabbey. Have you been there? It is a lovely quaint little village on the shore of Strangford Lough, lots of antiquing to do on the main street. I used to go there with my wife before she sadly passed away. Anyway, it's a very nice place to visit".

Did he just deliberately inform me that he is a widower? The situation was difficult to gauge. In any case it is clear that he is not one of those men whose life falls to pieces when their wife dies. He looked healthy and astute. Not like the helpless ones who have dinner made for them every night by one of their adult children and are perpetually distraught. I was once a palliative care nurse you see. I would often find myself going back to the houses of the women I had looked after to care for their heartbroken, dying husbands, usually within two years of their wife's passing.

I liked him. I liked the fact that he was volunteering in a charity shop. I liked his clean hands. The appealing image of us enjoying a cream tea after a happy morning pottering around Greyabbey formed in my mind. That could make life here a bit more interesting.

When I left the shop, it was only late afternoon but darkness was falling already. I could feel the burn of cold air on my skin, I was unaccustomed to it. The frigid weather re-enforced my impression of this small market town as a hostile place. It had been modernised, made ugly, almost beyond recognition since I left. Perspex shop signs in eye watering colours proclaimed 'Sandra's Fashions', 'Jewell's Gift Emporium' and 'Cozy Corner Café'. Splodges of trampled chewing gum lay fossilised in the tarmac. Worst of all, the people in the street looked poor, careworn, pale.

I wanted to scream at the thought of being trapped here. *Calm yourself Annie, have a coffee and get a grip. It was always going to be strange at the beginning.* I started reading Madam Bovary in the Cozy Corner Café and took my time before going home. I wanted to give my sister Brigid a little breathing space. We were still trying to find some sort of rhythm to living together again after all these years.

In the street just outside Brigid's house I could hear the muffled tinkling of Gymnopédie with its poignant pauses. When I entered the dining room she was sitting on the piano stool, long legs at right angles, her trousers were too short and they rode up quite a distance above her ankles exposing thick socks and suede slippers. She had stopped playing when she heard the key turn it the door.

"What did you do this afternoon?" asked Brigid with a solemn face.

"Well hello to you too! Can I take my coat off before we have a chat?"

After hanging my coat up in the hall I went into the kitchen to put the kettle on. Brigid followed me and sat by the small table that had once belonged in our childhood home. It took pride of place like all the inherited things in Brigid's house.   Polished and cherished.

Brigid lit a cigarette and drew on it greedily before saying through a plume of electric-blue smoke:

"You were seen flirting like a glipe with the man in the charity shop this afternoon."

Ambushed.

"What on earth are you talking about Brigid?"

She frowned making her eyes appear smaller. I had a sudden memory of our mother instructing in a sing-song voice, "eyebrows, Brigid, eyebrows!" to correct her grumpy appearance.

"He is a Protestant," she hissed.

"Nobody thinks like that anymore," I said and laughed a genuine laugh, "and besides I don't really know what this has to do with you".

"What would our mother and father think?"

"I am inclined not to care".

A flash of anger darted across Brigid's icy eyes and I detected a slight flaring of nostrils so I said in a conciliatory tone:

"Come on Brigid, how old are we?"

"Exactly. You are making an eejit out yourself mooning over a man at your age."

"Brigid what is wrong with you?"

Then I saw it coming. It had a tragic inevitability; the purging of ancient, molten vitriol.

"I shouldn't even have mentioned it. It won't make any difference. You have always suited yourself. I suppose I just hoped now that you are old you might conduct yourself with a bit more decorum. I shouldn't expect too much from someone who ran away pregnant to the other side of the world to hide their *love child*."

"Oh give me a break, Brigid. Would you have preferred it if Daddy had carted me off to the convent instead? Well, I didn't give him that chance. I wasn't about to let anyone steal my baby from me. This is all ancient history. By the way, that 'love child' is your niece and she has a name. *Ophelia*."

"Oh-feelie-ya", Brigid tilted her head to the side as she said it, relishing every syllable. The childish facial expression made her old face look grotesque. "What kind of name is that anyway?"

I wanted to slap her.

Rise above it.

"Ophelia is my family. I want to live near her. I can tell you now I wouldn't be back in this godforsaken place if she hadn't moved from Sydney to Belfast with my grandchildren.''

Take a deep breath.

"Do you know how homesick I was when I first left Ireland?" I said as quietly and with as much restraint as I could muster. "Do you think that was the easy option? I was terrified. I couldn't sleep at night unless I imagined I was walking up the steps from Main Street to our old house. I would count each of the steps in my mind."

"Daddy never knew the real reason why you left. It was a terrible time. His heart was broken. It nearly killed him!"

"It is a pity it didn't. He lived for another 20 years destroying our mother's life!"

There was a long pause. I had a sensation of walls closing in. These old houses are so solid, they interfere with the mind, the bricks and mortar are dense with history.

"I think it would be better if you moved out."

"Yes, so do I."

I grabbed my books off the table and stormed upstairs. I dozed briefly on top of the bed covers and dreamt that I was standing near Brigid while she played the piano but the playing was soundless. I could hear the background noise of the road outside, the small creaks of radiators and pipes, the grandfather clock was ticking but not even the dull thud of the piano pedals was audible. When I woke, I sat on the edge of the bed.

The old bat will need me soon enough.

I will not move out. I will stay here and look after her until the end. A quick snoop a few days ago at the medication she kept hidden in her bedroom had confirmed my suspicions. Brigid is dying of cancer. Liver cancer if my intuition is correct. I wonder when she will finally tell me.

I need distraction.

I opened the book on Buddhism and the first line said:

"No work for love will flourish out of guilt, fear, or hollowness of heart, just as no valid plans for the future can be made by those who have no capacity for living now."

I shut the book hard. Yes, once familiar books seem very different now.

"Nature Reclaims", by Brynnie Rafe

Their bicycle gears creaked and complained as they steered their way through the narrow streets, occasionally swerving to avoid a car. Neither of them had wanted to ride but there wasn't room in the car for everyone and at least they wouldn't be squashed into the centre of yet another fierce argument about who got to keep the grandfather clock. In fact, they'd even decided to ride over early to escape the calm-before-the-storm atmosphere of the house. One casual remark about something that Gran had done would be the spark that kindled the next argument and after that they would be powerless to stop the adults. Auntie Lois would cry and Auntie Katherine would snap and then Mum would shout at everyone to shut up but they wouldn't, their insults getting more and more vicious until they descended into a cacophony of jealousy and rage.

It had been like that ever since Gran had died three weeks ago and Lila wondered that the house hadn't fallen apart at the seams from all the turmoil inside. First Lois and her husband and their three children had arrived, their rosy faces splitting with grins and sugary compliments, laden with presents for Lila and Eddie until a reference to Gran's Turkish vase had cracked open Lois's false visage.

'We always picked the roses together.' she had whined, 'I can't believe that you'd be selfish enough to try and take that away from me. I'm surprised *you* even remember that vase.'

Then Auntie Katherine, her grey-brown tendrils of hair sticking up around her face like Medusa, accompanied by her brooding husband who hardly spoke but seemed to bang the table at regular intervals. She didn't even try and maintain a pretence of being nice.

'Do you think we came all the way from New Zealand just to visit you and your lovely family?' she leered sarcastically, 'I'm the oldest and I always knew Mum would want me to sort out her things, even if it means staying in your dump of a house until we can get hold of the keys to Preston Avenue.'

'You haven't got children to pass it on to!' interrupted cousin Hugh, who had somehow materialised during one of the arguments. 'What's the point of hoarding all her things just so they can gather dust in that Auckland house you're always bragging about?'

'Carly loves pretty things' simpered his wife, stroking her toddler's hair. 'That pearl necklace is just the sort of thing I dream of giving her to treasure when she's older.'

'Shut up!' somebody shouted, but Lila was already on her way to her room. Although it was infested with little cousins and Eddie was probably hiding under her bed, anything was better than that tormented atmosphere.

She'd considered not even coming to see the house at all but Gran's collection of antiques had always held a certain fascination for Lila. She tried to picture it the way she'd last seen it three years ago, before Gran had insisted that no one visit her: lawn clipped within an inch of its life, rose bushes of every colour and vines tamed by wrought iron gates. The stained glass windows near the door. The amazingly lifelike porcelain cats next to the fireplace.

Gran had announced three years ago that no one should come round to visit her anymore; she was going to shut up most of the rooms, she'd said, the house being too large for her, and she didn't want any more fighting over her things while she was still alive. When she'd had to move to a retirement home a year ago, no one could agree who was going to move in so they'd let it be. Apparently, Gran was hiring a cleaner to come in every week and dust the lonely sculptures and brush the velvet cushions on the 18th century dining chairs. It was believed that most of the furniture was lurking under dust-sheets. No one seemed to be able to face going over there until after the funeral and anyway, none of them had a set of keys so they'd waited until this lemon yellow Saturday morning to go and pack up Gran's things. There was, of course, the small matter of who would inherit the house, but the will wasn't clear and the single time it had come up in conversation, their house had emptied of people for three whole days. The relatives came swarming back like flies, however, after a couple of nights in their separate motels. At least no one mentioned the house after that. Perhaps their ears were still ringing from that foul altercation.

'Wait for me, Lila!' her little brother's voice jolted her back to reality. She braked softly and waited for him to catch up.

'What are we even going to do at Gran's house?' he moaned, 'It's gonna be *boring*.'

'You didn't have to come!' she retorted, 'Maybe you should ride back home and remind Auntie Lois how much you always loved the china cats.' Eddie whimpered.

'I'm sorry.' she sighed, 'I'm just so sick of everyone. Why don't we explore the garden, huh?' She didn't add that the garden never had a stick out of place and that disturbing it would invoke the wrath of their family.

They turned into a shady, tree-lined avenue, European-style houses gleaming white in the morning sun, dappled sunlight dancing on the pavement. The houses were much larger than the scruffy weatherboards and cheap modern flats in their part of town, they all looked like they belonged to some sort of royalty, set back from the road with elaborate porches and sometimes small turrets. The aroma of exotic flowers permeated the warm air. Petals from the cistus fluttered in the breeze. Fruits swelled on heavy branches. But for the persistent noise of traffic on the road they might have ridden into another world.

Lila braked and stopped the bike at a high stone wall draped with ivy. The ivy was certainly new, she thought, Gran would be turning in her grave to see her wall disfigured so. They walked along to the small lych-gate almost in the centre of the wall. It was a tall gate, Gran had always liked to have privacy, but Lila couldn't help noticing that there were vines woven through the cracks in the wood and roses hanging over the archway. She tried the latch.

'It's locked.' she said to Eddie.

'Can we go and get an ice-cream instead?'

She sighed.

'I don't have any money. Anyway, we can still climb over the wall and explore the garden, like I said.'

He looked disappointed.

'I'm sorry, Eddie. I really am, but I can't do anything about it. We might as well have a look around since we're here, though.'

Eddie nodded reluctantly. She straightened her bike against the wall and lifted him so he was standing on the seat.

'Hold the ivy and I'll give you a boost. Once you're up there you can tell me what you can see. It'll be like we're real explorers!'

'But we're not real explorers!'

'What happened to your imagination, huh? I thought little kids still liked playing imaginative games.'

'I'm not a little kid! I'm seven years old!'

'Whatever. Just climb up or I'll leave you outside.'

'Fine' said Eddie, in a voice that he probably thought was grown up but sounded distinctly brattish. You couldn't blame him considering how their family had been behaving. She lifted him up and he crawled along the ivy-topped wall.

'What can you see?'

'It's like a jungle!'

Lila raised her eyebrows. Surely Gran wouldn't have let the garden go completely. Didn't she have a gardener?

'Hang on, don't fall. I'm coming up.'

Gripping the ivy and pushing off her bike with her foot, she hoisted herself up. The bike clattered to the pavement but she ignored it. The streets were mostly deserted in this part of town anyway. She glanced over to check Eddie was alright and looked down into the garden.

It was a sea of green foliage. Banks of weeds were dotted with vibrant smudges of floral colour and the topiary animals had become monstrous creatures adorned with swaying tendrils. The ivy hung over everything: the hedges, the fountains, the greenhouse, the enormous oak tree whose acorns littered the ground. The once clear pond was choked with algae, yet the red waterlilies glowed like ripe fruit. Most of the trellises had fallen down and leaned at awkward angles, stepladders for the advancing greenery. The perfume of the honeysuckle was pungent and sweet, the flowers jostling for space on the vines. Around the great apple tree there was a smattering of windfalls that looked like discarded baubles. The garden had flourished in Gran's absence, the dense vegetation almost hiding the house from view.

'Wow' breathed Lila, 'Wow.'

'I didn't know Gran's garden was like this!' said Eddie. Butterflies landed on his fair hair, drunk with nectar.

'Neither did I' laughed Lila, sliding off the wall and into the thicket below. 'Come on! Now we will be real explorers! Real enough, anyway.'

Stalks of grass whipped her legs and thorns snagged in her hair as she raced through overgrown roses. Eddie followed her, tripping over grasping vines but stumbling on, up what had once been the path up to the house.

'I bet the front door's locked' she said, surveying the grubby white facade. The ivy clung to the white porch columns like clothing and coiled around the topmost window frames. 'We'll go round the back, see what we can find!'

She was gripped by a sort of childish excitement as if every overgrown hollow could yield a new secret. She laughed again and swept back garlands of leaves that glowed in the sun. She skipped over daisies and buttercups, swung under the branches of the great oak tree whose branches might have held a whole world.

'Lila?' came Eddie's inquisitive voice. She turned around.

'What is it?'

'How come all these windows are open?'

She frowned, sobered.

'What do you mean they're open?'

'They're open! Look!'

She looked up. Sure enough, each window had been methodically opened, the curtains flung aside revealing the dim rooms within. She stood on her tiptoes and looked inside.

It had been a living room once, it was clear, with a large chandelier and shelves of Gran's vintage book collection, as well as her blown glass bottle collection but the Persian carpet was littered with leaves and Lila could hear the twittering of birds from the bookshelf. The chandelier sported a veil of ivy and the blue ceiling was turning green from dampness. A few weeds grew between the cracks in the floorboards.

'What the...?' she whispered under her breath. There were no signs of dust-sheets on anything. It was almost as if nature had received an invitation. She crept along to the next room, almost furtive, as if something could be living inside. Silk cushions had been ripped apart to make nests for birds. A velvety carpet of moss covered the floor and lichen adorned the walls like a strangely abstract fresco. A glass lamp lay shattered in amongst the weeds. There was no sign of any recent human presence. A few red toadstools were growing in a patch of dirt near the window.

'Is this even Gran's house?' asked Eddie, who had caught up with her.

'Of course it is!' Eddie, Lila realised, probably didn't remember visiting this house.

'Why's it all wrecked?'

Lila shrugged and then shivered. The dilapidated house was eerily silent but for the twittering of birds. The rusty shutters groaned softly as they swung on their hinges and the whispers of leaves suddenly seemed sinister.

'I don't know... let the adults figure that out when they get here. Shall we go and get some apples?'

An hour later they were lying under the huge apple tree, mouths sticky with apple juice. Lila licked her lips and looked towards the ivy-covered fountain. The hands of a stone nymph reached up, making a futile attempt to escape the weeds.

'I think Gran must have left the house open herself...' she mused. 'Before she left, I mean. She always hated how everyone argued over her stuff and I remember her saying something once...' Her voice trailed off.

'What did she say?' asked Eddie.

Lila thought back to that evening, four summers ago. She'd been lying on the couch with her eyes closed in one of the sitting rooms and the adults had all forgotten she was there. They were arguing, of course. Gran was clearly getting tired of it and kept trying to change the subject.

'You kids, always fighting over my old junk. Sometimes I think I'd better let it go to ruin, rather than let you all squabble over it when I'm gone. That'd teach you, wouldn't it? I won't have my legacy be a family quarrel.'

'Something about how she'd rather let the house go to ruin than have them argue over it.' Lila continued, 'I guess I thought it was a joke to try and make them stop arguing but now... It couldn't have been burglars, they'd have taken a lot more stuff and anyway, what sort of burglar leaves every window open? She had a cleaner but how do we know she was still paying them? I always thought it was kind of weird how she never invited us round, I mean I know she was protective about her collection but you'd think she would have had the adults round sometimes or invited us for Christmas... And when *I* was little I was always allowed to visit.' Eddie frowned, as if trying to comprehend what his sister was saying.

'Mum said that Taylor spilt lemonade on Gran's special rug and she got mad and then we weren't allowed to go to her house anymore,' he offered.

'Yeah, that's true, but I just don't know why else it's all open and creepy. The cleaners would have closed it if she was still paying them. Maybe she left something in the bit that's still locked up, like a letter. I don't know, this is like something out of a movie.'

'We could go and look for the letter.'

She smiled. 'I don't have the keys. Anyway, we should probably keep out of the way when Auntie Lois gets here.' She giggled. 'I guess this'll just have to be our little mystery.'

Lila lay back, watching the sunlight sparkling through the leaves. The whispers of the leaves were no longer scary, just a companion to the quiet she had craved for weeks. She closed her eyes and sighed. The garden, she decided, was better wild. Before it had been stifling in its perfection, nature caged and tamed to entertain and please the human eye. Now it was itself again, wild and yet strangely beautiful. Flourishing.

She hoped that Gran had meant to leave it like this, to let it go back to its roots now she no longer needed it, to let nature take the house and let the vines grow over the old prejudices and enmities. Maybe the adults would fight over this, she thought, but they'd agree on one thing.

'It's such a shame,' they'd all say, 'Such a lovely house and look at it now.'

Which was exactly what Lila wanted to do.

'I'll bring the camera one day,' she thought, 'This would make a stunning photography project.'

'They're here, Lila!' said Eddie, 'I can hear them.'

'Sssh...' She put a finger to her lips. 'We don't want to be found.'

He smiled, as if it was their special secret. She heard the footsteps on the pavement and the groaning of the gate as someone forced it open, their loud voices intruding on their place of peace.

'Wait til they see it, Eddie' she whispered, and laughed softly. 'Just you wait.'

In a hundred years the house might just be a heap of hedges and brambles, columns cracked and windows broken, fountains buried under a shroud of nettles, regardless of whether anyone restored it now. In a thousand years it might just be dust, an ancient relic of a time gone by crumbled away to nothing. Lila pictured the fountain nymphs face, cracked and disfigured like an ancient roman statue, staring out of the ground, half-buried. She imagined children flitting in and out of the ruins, laughing like her and Eddie had laughed. No one would quarrel over it or ransack its rooms, hungry for anything of value. Why not let nature do what it always sets out to do: reclaim its own? They were only delaying the inevitable.

'One day, it will gone,' she thought. 'But in the meantime, it's kind of extraordinary.'

"Homebloom", by Anthony Sweet

Janey opened the door in empty air. No one that walked past noticed the frame of frangipani and orchid blooms. When she closed the door behind them, the flowers cascaded to the floor and were trampled by a dozen weary feet.

It was her greatest trick, and Beth was the only one to see it.

"Do you like magic?" said the woman two seats down, popping an olive in her mouth. She was the only other person Beth had seen regularly outside of her new workmates. The office was cramped and overflowing with eagerness and lunchtime smells. This bar had become her respite; from the daily Skype calls back to San Francisco; from the language barriers with her forty new employees; from this wholly alien place.

Beth picked at her sandwich. An ambitious lettuce leaf flopped out. "Sure, I guess."

"Watch this." The woman picked up two toothpicks and held them between her thumb and forefinger. A quick pass of her hand in front of the other, and the two toothpicks now proudly bore an olive each, impaled through the centres.

"Neat," said Beth. "Mind passing me the picks?"

The woman slid the shaker up the bar. "New here?" she asked.

"Three weeks." Three weeks of little sleep, of server rooms and meetings and desperately failing at Chinese pronouns.

"Quick tip; cover your mouth," said the stranger. She put both impaled olives in her mouth and slid the toothpicks out. "Cultural thing."

"Oh," said Beth, embarrassed. "Thanks."

"You should come see my show."

"You're a performer?" said Beth. "Where and when?"

The woman left money on the bar and stood up. "You'll figure it out. Or I'll see you here tomorrow."

Beth should have felt annoyed, but honestly, she was just glad to speak face-to-face English for a few minutes.

"Be honest Beth, you hate the job."

The concrete floor was cold through her pants, and her cardigan was scrunched up in a corner of the room. Her mobile phone was wedged between her shoulder and ear, while a wireless handset tinkled elevator music in the other. She typed with her one spare hand, trying to remember which of the asset servers was named *dilly*.

"I don't hate the job, mum. I mean, there's always things that could be improved. It'd be nice to unpack my suitcase at some stage. And sure, I could do to crack some sense through my producer's thick skull and oh god afternoon I mean good afternoon Robert how are you?" She dropped the mobile into her typing hand and hung up on her mother.

"It's one in the morning, Beth. What do you want?"

"The secondary assets server crashed, and I can't bring it back up as a shared drive."

"So call the tech guys."

"No one's picking up, just like last week. Why do we bother having nerds on-call if they can't roll out of their Cheeto daze when we need them?"

"I'll talk to them in the morning."

"Robert, I have forty animators about to walk right now."

There was a moment's pause for late night calculations. "It's afternoon there, right? Give them an early night for once."

"Milestone delivery is in two days."

"See, I didn't know that on account of my thick skull."

Beth winced. "This network is a mess, I'm not even convinced our backups are covering all of the repos. We can't keep patching with bandaids and hope for the best. Can I bring in someone local?"

"I'm not paying for it." The dial tone sounded louder than it had any right to be. Beth dropped the wireless handset on the concrete floor, where it failed to break into satisfying pieces of cheap plastic.

She didn't hate the job. Theoretically this was her dream; abroad in an exotic country, creative work on a summer blockbuster, her name in the credits as a studio lead. On paper, the job was perfect.

A head poked in through the doorway. Wesley, self-appointed team spokesman, smiled down at her. "All good?"

"No, Wesley, not all good. I need someone to come in and look at this mess. Do you know anyone?"

"Ah, network admin? Sure, sure. My brother, he could come in and look at it."

"Does he know what he's doing?"

Wesley was already doing thumb gymnastics on his phone. "You mean, is he a professional?"

"Yeah."

"No."

Beth sighed. "When can he come in?"

"Mmm. Tomorrow."

A small troupe of footfalls marched past. Wesley turned around and cheerfully said his goodbyes in Cantonese.

"Was that my B-team?"

"And half of Admin."

"What? Why are they going?"

"They have finished their lunch."

"Yes, but why are they… ugh, whatever. Did they clean up the kitchen at least?"

Wesley looked down the hall. "Mmm. No. See you tomorrow, boss."

Beth returned her glare to the monitor. An error message cheerily flashed back. *External drive "dilly" not found.*

The perfect job on paper.

The 90's grunge soundtrack conflicted with the bar's faux black marble interior. In the week she'd been coming here for lunch, Beth had never noticed any kind of midday rush, and had yet to see anyone sat behind the baby grand plonked indelicately by the large street-facing windows. Today, she doubled the lunchtime crowd.

"You didn't find me," said the woman.

"Work was busy," lied Beth. She had tried scouting two of the casinos closest to home, but found no sign her lunch companion. "Have a good show?"

"Eh," shrugged the woman. "About usual."

Beth sat down on a stool next to the woman, and quietly scanned the menu for a minute before ordering a club sandwich with the bartender. The man nodded and disappeared into the kitchen.

"So, my name's Beth," she said, interrupting the pregnant silence between them. "I work for an animation studio."

"Like, cartoons?"

"More like special effects."

"Strange place for that. You're from Australia, right?"

"Melbourne, then San Fran. Now, here."

"China's Las Vegas," smirked the woman.

Her phone buzzed, another angry text from one of the IT supports back at the bay. They weren't happy about Wesley's brother restructuring their network hierarchy. He had worked quick, with everything back online half an hour before the rest of the studio had arrived. By lunchtime, Beth had handed him a colourful stack of notes from the petty cash tin and told him to call it a day, but the kid seemed happy tinkering in the stuffy server room. No data was going out, no login failures; the tech team had nothing to complain about, except for the fact that a twenty year old was doing their job for them.

"Speaking of Vegas, you got a new trick for me?"

"Sure." She held up a coin, one of the local ones with the gold-coloured centre, and slowly, deliberately, removed her fingers until the coin was left hanging mid-air between them.

Beth looked up from floating coin to find the magician looking straight back. "Where are you performing tonight?"

"Same as last night," said the woman.

"No clues?"

The coin was snapped up between thumb and forefinger. "Don't think too hard about it. We foreigners tend to be creatures of habit."

Beth looked down at her freshly delivered club sandwich. It was her fourth for the week.

The remaining afternoon passed in a predictable blur. Both animation teams lagged as the clock inched towards closing, and the admin team packed up soon after completing payroll. The emails from support complaining about Wesley's brother doing their job for them eased up once it hit midnight back home.

She locked the doors at 8:10. Beth wanted to go and find her magician friend, but she was already tired, and the coming morning promised missed deadlines and extended conference calls.

The hotel bar was on the way home. Maybe a quiet drink before bed.

The faux marble looked a lot more glamorous under the disguise of night and the reflection of casino lights. Heavy mauve curtains that were always drawn aside during the day were invitingly slung half open along the window front. Inside, a dozen people stood at dimly lit tables, talking fondly over martini glasses and scotch tumblers.

The magician sat at the piano, the cheshire of a grin teasing Beth through the glass.

Beth felt severely underdressed as she walked in. Tinkly jazz melodies washed over her.

"When you said you were a performer, I thought you meant as a magician," said Beth, watching the hands on the piano.

"Nah, there's no money in magic. Easier to just tinkle some two-fives for the tourists. More free drinks, too."

"Free drinks? I'm in the wrong business."

The piano player nodded to a couple as they walked past, and wound up the jazz standard with a flourish up the ladder of keys. "Any requests?"

"I don't really know much jazz," said Beth apologetically.

The woman started playing again. It sounded lovely and complex to Beth. It made her wish that she'd spent more time as a kid in front of the piano instead of watching cartoons.

"Janey," said the woman.

"Is that this song?"

"My name."

"Oh," said Beth, embarrassment creeping up her neck. "Maybe I should--"

"Sit down?" said Janey with a smile. "My set's nearly over."

Beth nodded, and walked the dark edge of the room to the bar. The same bartender who served her lunch brought her bourbon and ice, and she sat alone with the couples and the piano player.

They talked about music, and drinks, and the night life of this strange island. They reminisced like old friends and yet remained strangers. Beth admitted that she still lived out of her single tightly packed suitcase, and Janey talked excitedly about the scooter she'd bought third-hand from a drummer in Hong Kong.

Beth left the bar soon after 10:00, and wallowed in the strangeness of living abroad. Outside of the office, in the times she had to herself, it was all very strange and unreal.

Black and white cobblestones reflected the neon colours of gambling and decadence, of consumer electronics and imported fast food. Then the cobblestones gave way to sidewalk cement as she reached her familiar apartment building.

The sirens and dumpy blue security cars were new, though. Clothes were scattered across the road, punctuated by broken glass. Beth counted the windows and felt her heart sink; the smashed window was on the third floor.

"Senhorita?" A uniform gently stepped in her way. "Senhorita , você mora aqui?"

"What? Uh… fala… English? Inglese?"

"Oh. Miss, do you live here?" The police woman spoke English, but she didn't appear to like doing so.

Beth nodded. "I live up there." She looked over the destruction littered across the road. "That, that's my suitcase. Those are my clothes they're picking up!"

"You need to come with me. It was a big break-in."

It took half an hour for Beth to collect her belongings off the street and shove them into her broken suitcase. Once done, she quietly catalogued everything that was missing from her barely lived in room upstairs: two pairs of shoes; jewellery; spare change tin; her documents folder with visa, passport, insurance details.

The police woman had tried to be helpful, but there wasn't much she could do. Beth would have to go to the Immigration Department in the morning and sort out her missing visa paperwork. And she'd need to talk to her insurance, except she didn't have the number saved in her phone, and Robert wasn't answering her calls, and the window and door would need repairing but the landlord didn't want to know about it until the morning and--

She was alone now in the destroyed apartment. Her mobile dialled out, and Robert's voicemail started again. Beth threw the phone out the broken window. There was an unsatisfying crack as it hit the bitumen three stories down.

"I'm not going to cry," she told herself, feeling the contrary starting to well up. "I'm not giving them the satisfaction. I'm not."

She grabbed the handle of her battered suitcase. The grip twisted and snapped off in her hand.

Beth left her apartment and belongings, open and defiled, with only her handbag and a spare sweater wrapped over her shoulders.

It wasn't until she was walking past the piano bar that she realised she was on autopilot. Of course, Janey sat at the piano by the window.

Of course, she'd already seen Beth.

Beth wanted to walk right past. Humiliation and frustration knotted her stomach.

Janey met her at the door, and Beth walked right into the hug and sobbed. She barely knew this woman, who patted her hair and sat her down in the emptying bar. When Beth lifted her head for breath, the room was empty except the bartender.

"I've, I've, I've already spoken to the police," was the first thing Beth said.

"You're alright then?"

Beth took a deep breath. "My apartment was trashed."

"Ah damn. That's rough."

"It's only been three weeks, you know?" She wiped her face on a thoroughly soaked tissue, and gratefully accepted a fresh napkin. "Coming here was supposed to be a good thing. All I ever wanted was to work in animation. You get an opportunity to lead a studio somewhere in China, you take it, right?"

"It's not a dream if it's working for someone else," Janey said eventually. "Other people don't leave you room to grow. Your glass ceiling is a conference call thirteen hours away."

"Fifteen." Beth sighed, ragged with regret. "I wish I never came here."

"Do you need somewhere to stay?"

Beth shook her head. "Thanks, but I've got a night bag at the studio."

"At least let me walk you there," said Janey.

They said their goodbyes out the front of the commercial block, and Beth unlocked the studio. She shut her laptop, ignoring the dozen unread notifications, and fumbled in the dark for the sports bag with her spare clothes and toothbrush.

Wrapped in her sweater, her duffel bag her pillow and the night finally behind her, Beth fell asleep.

"Boss? Boss?" said Wesley. Beth opened her eyes. Morning light already filled the room. "Elizabeth?"

"Wesley? What time is it?"

"Half past nine. Are you okay?"

"I had a rough night." Beth sat up, sluggish. Her face felt creased from spending the night smooshed against the duffel bag.

Wesley closed the door behind him. "My brother did not do it."

"Do what?" said Beth. "Wesley, why are you whispering?"

"Stephen is not the leak!"

"Leak? What are you talking about?"

Wesley looked concerned, and then surprised. "You do not know?"

"I had a really bad night last night. Just tell me what's wrong."

Wesley made a sound that was half sigh and half groan as he opened the laptop. Twenty seconds tapping on the keyboard, and he spun the laptop around for Beth to see from her spot on the floor. It was a familiar scene, a render from one of the action sequences the studio had been working on before she had arrived. It took her a moment longer to realise it was attached to a news article. The headline accused her in 22 point font, with words like 'top secret' and 'leaked'.

Wesley clicked a link.

There was video embedded into the article. Youtube stamp in the bottom corner. A fully rendered twenty second scene.

"What… how did this…" They were months away from being able to show this footage. The production company had a PR firm on standby waiting for this very scene. The campaign budget was in the millions.

This leak was going to cost her her job.

"It was not Stephen. I promise. He is not this stupid," said Wesley.

"Well, who was it then, Wesley? He didn't sign an NDA." Beth groaned and rolled onto her back. "I forgot to give him the NDA."

"It wasn't him. We will find out who."

"And then what, lynch mob?" Beth stared at the ceiling. Damp stains and cracks. "The damage is already done, Wesley. Just… I don't know. Go do something. Leave me alone."

Wesley closed the door behind him. The laptop pinged with another notification, an email with more exclamation marks than words.

Beth closed her eyes.

Her inbox pinged again.

She'd never felt this alone before.

For the first time, Beth walked into the piano bar and had no one to sit next to. The room was empty except for the bartender.

"Do you even sleep?" she asked the man behind the bar, who just smiled.

Her club sandwich was mostly finished when Janey walked in. "You don't look so good."

"Don't suppose you've got a Get Out Of Jail Free card up that sleeve," said Beth between final mouthfuls.

"Something happen at Immigration?"

"Haven't been."

"You don't want to mess around with this, Beth."

"What's it matter?" said Beth. "Haven't even got the cash to pay for breakfast."

"Forget about that. Are you leaving?"

"Don't see how. No money, no passport. Got nothing to do but head back to the office and pick up what's left of my career."

Janey looked down at the empty plate, then back up to Beth. "Come with me."

Beth took the woman's hand and let her be led out into the sunlight. The square was bustling, vendors and tourists alike edging past each other. Janey took her out to the middle of the black and white cobblestones. The crowds flowed around the pair, a pedestrian stream around two rocks.

"Are you happy here?"

"What? No," said Beth. "But whatever. I'll work it out. Maybe I can figure something out with Robert--"

From nowhere, Janey opened the door of flowers. "Are you happy here?" Janey repeated.

"No," said Beth. "I'm really not."

Janey held out a hand. "Then let's go."

The door closed behind them. The flowers fell to the floor, trampled   and   forgotten.

"Jettisoned", by Vickie Walker

It's an old wooden jetty. Been in our town for over a hundred years. My grandfather helped cart the timber they used to build it down from the forests. He was 15 at the time - a boy doing a man's work. Grandpa told me stories of ships that plied the coast, ships that carried our timber to places further afield and others that came with supplies. Like many lads, he dreamed of joining one of the ships and sailing to exotic destinations; or even, to go to the big city, a faraway wonder in itself.

This jetty has our history embedded in its woodgrain; it's why we exist as a town. The rails, the timber, it's rough. She's dilapidated, but as solid as the day it was built. Those men knew how to make something to last.

We use it; there's scuff marks from a thousand feet. Paint on the railing's chipped in places; arms and feet rest on it every day. And wind, sand and sea have done their best to wear her down.

Yet she's special. Most of us come here each day to walk, think and people watch. Old women come to stroll, arms linked, heads close, reliving old days. Old men fish off the end of the jetty, tossing lines into blue-grey water, never seeming to catch anything. Young boys, knee deep in water at low tide, drag fingers through seaweeds which flourish here, stirring up tiny creatures living there. People walking, people thinking, people living.

Boats at anchor rock like cradles, water lapping at their sides. Others drift at sea; specks of white, red, blue. They're purely for fun now; no timber is shipped out anymore, hasn't been for a long time. Not since the railroad was built. Then later, there was no timber. Our town's not as big as it once was, in its heyday. We like it that way.

The jetty is the town, the town is the jetty. So why are the Council letting bloody developers in? They want to pull it down and build a fancy steel and concrete monstrosity, a modern marina, just to pull rich tourists in. They even want outdoor cafes. Our town doesn't need all that. People come here for peace and quiet, to get away from the city and the to-ing and fro-ing. If they want cafes they can go somewhere else. Besides the bakery does a damn good cappuccino.

Well, I won't stand for it. If they think they can march in and railroad us into letting them do what they like, they can think again. Action stations! That's what we need to do. Action stations.

"Quiet please! Everyone quiet!" I yell over the din and babble filling the hall. "If you could all take your seats, we'll get started." I wait until the crowd shuffles onto chairs and settles.

"Right. I call to order the first meeting of the 'Save Our Jetty' campaign. As you are aware Maddison Point Developers are proposing to demolish our jetty to replace it with a marina complex. We're here today to form a committee to fight against the development." My greying hair fell into my eyes. I'm nervous; this public speaking isn't my thing.

"Here, here," from the audience.

"We need nominations from three or four of you to join me on this committee, so if you have the time and energy for the fight ahead, raise your hand now."

I scan the faces in front of me. I'm known to most of them; family's been in the area for generations; I'm a local who's worked and lived here and raised my kids. Lucky I retired recently. I wouldn't have had the time when I was a carpenter.

A lot of townsfolk are here. They seem keen to hear what I plan to do. Many are edgy of change to our little community, yet with no idea how to stop it.

Several men and women raise their hands, Pat Simcox the butcher; Shaz Derby a housewife; and Marie Lennox, the local solicitor. I note it's a good cross-section, and I'm pleased to see

Marie involved, her skills will be useful. This meeting is the first step in a long hard fight.

My wife isn't keen when I tell her what I'm doing after the meeting.

"Why can't someone else do it?" Jean asks.

"We all need to help. We're a small community. Numbers are essential."

"Humph," she said. "You're a fool Matt Granger, always a big softie at heart."

We meet next evening in the pub. Marie is there when I arrive.

"I'm glad to have your input," I tell her. "I think we'll come up against some weighty arguments."

Marie sips her wine. "These developers usually have an army of lawyers. My experience is purely local you know, but I'm rearing for the fight."

"You weren't born here, so why do you want to help?"

"I love that jetty; it's my peace and quiet when I stroll there to watch the sunset. I know others feel the same. It's worth saving."

Pat and Shaz arrive.

"Let's get down to business." I'm eager to move things along. Jean likes dinner on time.

I'm elected President, Shaz Secretary, the Treasurer/Fundraiser is Pat and Marie became our legal advisor. We call the group 'SOJ' for 'Save Our Jetty'.

"Council is calling for submissions about the Development Application. They close in six weeks so we need to act fast." I scratch my head. "Any ideas?"

Pat's a direct bloke. "I vote for a letter drop to all residents. Not everyone knows about the submissions."

"Yes," Shaz agrees. "I know someone at the paper. She has kids at school. I'll get her to write an article."

"We must send an official letter to Council to let them know we exist and that we will be protesting against this development," Marie notes.

I knew, with our town being part of a larger shire, most Councillors didn't live in the town. Only one, Shane Jackson, did and he was keen on the development. "There's a Council meeting early next month. I'll go and follow up on our letter so Shaz, tell them I want to speak at the meeting."

"OK. I'll get letters to the residents copied. If we could meet to distribute them Saturday arvo?"

All is agreed and I arrive home in time for dinner.

Saturday is busy, putting letters in mailboxes. I hope they stir the community into action, into writing submissions, into protest. Already the developers are pushing the 'good' of their cause in the papers and on TV. They're a big conglomerate with money and power, pushing the town's growth.

Their representative, John Babcock, seems a decent bloke when I meet with him two days later.

"This town needs jobs," he said as we sit down for a beer. "It's dying. Families are moving away or having to travel to the larger centres for work."

"The figures aren't as alarming as you're painting," I protest. "And we're working on ways to improve that, without destroying our jetty."

"The marina will guarantee jobs for a long time. Surely that's a good thing."

I know what he means. Those out of work see this as a positive. It's hard to argue for an old jetty when people don't have a job. Yet I sense the jetty is important.

Even my wife queries the time I give to the cause.

"I thought when you retired, we'd travel," Jean complains. "All you do is eat, breathe and think about the jetty."

"It's just for a while," I soothe her. 'When we win, I'll relax."

"If you win Matt," she said. "If."

"No if about it." I'm firm. No good to be negative even around Jean. Not even to myself can I admit that defeat is the more likely outcome, especially when my talk to the Council goes down like a lead balloon.

We distribute leaflets on submission writing. We answer constant phone calls and emails as to what people should write. They seem interested but writing a submission is hard work; their time's limited, a thousand other things take priority. Most are writing about their own experience of the jetty, how they fished from it or tied their tinny there. Many of their grandfathers worked on it at some time or other, loading the ships. Their lives are tied up with jetty life.

Marie brings along to a meeting a copy of the government's National Heritage Listing rules. She hopes to find value in the jetty that needs protection.

"We have seaweed; it flourishes out near the end of the jetty. I've seen plenty of marine life," I said. "The DA says they'll dredge the bay to deepen it, so bigger boats can come in. It'll destroy the area."

"Mmm…not sure if we have any special fish or anything though."

"That strip of native bush," Shaz adds. "That's to be ripped out. I'm sure that's important, plenty of birds nest there each year. Who's that bloke, Pat? The one who comes each year to see the birds? He might know something."

Leaning back, Pat frowns. "Yeah I know, stays with Bob. I'll get onto it."

Despite the ideas and work, I despair about there being enough submissions lodged to make a difference. We're a small community, our number limited. What can we do against a company with big money? Advertisements appear in the paper and on TV proclaiming the wonder of the new development. Our group has no funds for ads.

People bail me up in the street. "Don't you want me to have a job?" they say. Or "My kids are leaving town, there's no work." I try to explain but I've got no answers for that problem. The destruction of marine life or birds or the jetty means less to these people than the need of a job.

I can't get Councillors to listen to me, to hear what I have to say. Too busy at present, Mayor Brown says. Can we meet next week? My emails remain unanswered; my phone calls aren't returned. Days rush by.

However there's a glimpse of optimism. Others are getting vocal, phoning Councillors, writing letters to the paper. A petition's raised and placed in the butcher's shop for people to sign.

Pat decides we need a protest march, complete with banners, to lodge the petition with our local Member, Tony Lederman. "The TV'll be here," he said. "Let's take advantage of that."

I'm unsure if people will attend in the numbers needed to make an impact. Ours is a conservative town; this is way off our radars. Yet we have to try, submissions close next month. Besides, some Councillors will be there, schmoozing with the politician. It might help turn them.

A week later, I'm at the hall. I'd spent the day before painting banners. 'Save Our Jetty' 'Don't destroy our past'. Jean decided that she'd join in. "I'm glad you see my point," I tell her.

"I figured it means a lot to you, your grandfather being involved."

"It's not that Jean. It's our town, not some big company's. We should have our say."

"I know. Let's see how many come today."

People arrive, in dribs and drabs, numbers build slowly. Children come, with cardboard signs, painted in thick black letters; mothers arrive pushing prams and strollers, balloons tied to the handles; there are older men and women, some on walking sticks. Young boys run about, handing out banners. There's a buzz, an excitement - a party atmosphere.

I stand in front of them, so proud of my town at that moment. "We'll march to the jetty. Our Member is meeting the developers there. We'll show them where we stand on this issue. SAVE OUR JETTY!" I shout.

The chant goes up, "SAVE OUR JETTY!" as our group forges along the road, banners high, a wave of colour and emotion. I lead the way with the committee.

At the jetty I see Tony Lederman, the local Member, shaking hands with John Babcock and others from the developers. Mayor Brown is there and Shane Jackson. A TV crew is filming.

The crowd chants louder. "We want our jetty!" "Hands off our jetty!"

I walk up to the Member. "We'd like to present this petition to you." Cameras turn to catch my image and that of the people behind me.

RESIDENTS RALLY TO SAVE THEIR JETTY. Headlines leap from the paper next day. I can't believe how many turned out, how enthusiastic they were. The reward - media coverage in our favour at last. That night I'm even on the news!

Letters of support come in. Letters from past visitors who'd enjoyed the jetty's ambience, who came because of the peacefulness of the area. A Marine Biologist, Mark Moore, arrives and spends two days taking samples, poking around the jetty. He leaves without giving us much hope though.

The amateur bird watcher is located and provides a list of nesting birds. He's optimistic and will add his own submission. The patch of bush is small but significant to many species in the area.

Still the developers push their cause. John is around town all the time. "Jobs," he proclaims. "Jobs." He tells the media that the Marina is environmentally sound; plans include protecting the coastal surrounds.Marie digs up an article suggesting that previous promises failed, where a resort in Queensland faced serious ecological issues. John counteracts that, stating that new procedures are in place.

Visitors come to see the jetty at the centre of the uproar. Each morning another tourist arrives, wanting information. I'm an unofficial tour guide, detailing the town's timber and shipping history.

"Why don't you put this jetty on your website?" One asks me. "I knew nothing of it until I saw it on TV."

"We don't have a website," I said. "Not much here for tourists."

"You kidding mate? People love old things like this."

I seek out the team. "What do you think of that?"

Marie's keen. "I've been checking out the heritage listing argument, we could have a case, both for the jetty's historical significance and bird life."

"Then we'd have something people would come to see. We could have more jobs that way, without destroying our town's history." I'm excited.

The submission date comes and goes. I've no idea how many are lodged. Now we wait. We continue to lobby the Councillors, hoping for votes in our favour.

It takes another fortnight before we discover that a record number of submissions have forced Council to nominate a neutral Convener to investigate further. People are invited to the hall to add to their submissions and answer questions from the Convener.

The committee and I sit at the front. I'm quite emotional outlining the case for the 'SOJ' committee. The Convener, Jane Simpson, is interested in what the amateur bird watcher had to say. She asks me if a qualified ornithologist verified the information.

"Not until next week," I tell her. "But the watcher is positive he's found something unique." Nodding, Jane moves to the next speaker.

A mum stands and tells of her boys who regard the jetty as their playground. Another speaks of his great-grandfather building the jetty. All ages, all backgrounds, all have something they want to share. The meeting stretches out, but no one cares. We have a jetty to save, our jetty.

John Babcock speaks for the developers. "Our plans will not only provide secure employment options, but we will do so with concern for the sensitive environment. We've had problems in the past, but new methods and procedures are in place. We are confident that all issues can be resolved."

Two Councillors attend but say nothing. They are here merely to observe.

The Convener ends the day. "My report goes to Council at the end of the week. I can assure you that all points of view have been noted."

I left, feeling that people had their say.

Marie phones me two days later. "The Marine Biologist just called. You know, Mark, who came up and poked around the jetty? He's found some new species of seaweed which flourish out there. He's thrilled by the whole thing. He's writing immediately to Council and Tony Lederman."

I'm elated. "Well, that's good news!"

"Yes, he says dredging would destroy the eco-system and wipe it out."

"Council votes next week."

"He says he'll be at the meeting, to give us his support."

I put down the phone and hug Jean, who is hovering around to hear what's going on.

"Looks like we've found our solution. A bit of seaweed, who'd have thought it!"

A week later, Council chambers are packed. Everyone wants to hear the decision about the jetty. The word is out about the seaweed and the biologist who will attend.

The Councillors file in, all is quiet. The usual proceedings dealt with, it's time for the item we're all interested in.

Mark Moore stands. "I've located a new species of *Scytothalia dorycarpa*. It is unique," he said. "I've approached the EPA and other authorities for its protection. I ask that you vote to save the jetty, as it is at the deepest parts of the jetty that the seaweed flourishes. The Development Application should be denied on environmental grounds."

People murmur amongst themselves. Councillors look at each other and at John Babcock.

Council votes. The vote is unanimous. The Development Application is denied. Mayor Brown stands, "It seems that this jetty is more important than we realised. We will investigate heritage listing, to protect this area of environmental significance."

Cheers and wolf whistles drown out the Mayor's final words. As the meeting adjourns, I see John Babcock leaving and turn to my team.

"Sneaking out," Pat's grin is as wide as his girth.

Shaz and Marie laugh. "Jettisoned, you mean."

I have to agree.

The laughter swirls around me as the townsfolk celebrate their win.

"More Flourish", by Joanna Watts

Miss Valentina's dance school boasted *authentic ballet instruction in the Kirov Ballet School tradition.* Marigold had no clue whether the ballet instruction was authentically Russian but Miss Valentina certainly was. She danced like a butterfly, graceful and light as she showed them how to do a perfect pirouette, a fabulous fouetté or an amazing arabesque. Even a simple plié looked like a work of art when Miss V demonstrated it. It took your breath away to see the human body jump and spin with such grace and precision.

But her elegance did not extend to her linguistic ability. She spoke English like a boxer: brutal, blunt, her words truncated and completely lacking in finesse and eloquence. When she became excited or more usually exasperated at her pupils lack of ability, she abandoned English altogether. Torrents of Russian streamed from her lips like a waterfall as her arms gesticulated wildly. The babble would eventually subside and Miss Valentina would compose herself once more and say with a sigh....

"Nu vot.....let'z try zat again shall we...zis time wiz more flourish."

'More flourish' was a perennial request but Marigold never could figure out what Miss V wanted from her pupils in response to it. No matter how hard she tried to give it *more flourish* Miss Valentina was not satisfied. Judging by the muttered comments from Jarrod, the one and only boy in the class, who stood next to Marigold at the barre, she was not alone in her confusion.

"More flourish.....More flourish" he repeated over and over one day. He spoke sotto voce but it was nevertheless a perfect imitation of Miss Valentina's heavily accented English, "More flourish....all I can ever think about when she says that is Harry Potter."

"Harry Potter?" Marigold couldn't resist turning around to look quizzically at Jarrod.

"Yes, you know....Flourish and Blotts: the bookshop in Diagon alley!"

Marigold giggled which was a big mistake. Miss Valentina ceased her demonstration of the correct way to transition from second to third position and was over to them in a flash.

"Oy, devochka, eta oozhas prosto....." The rant was on. Marigold felt her cheeks burn as Miss V lobbed her verbal grenades. Talking in class was considered a serious crime; on a par with turning up without correct dance uniform, or having failed to capture ones hair satisfactorily in a restrained bun with the requisite black ribbon around it. Marigold was often guilty of a dilapidated bun – her hair was too curly to sit obediently in a top knot – but talking was not usually an issue for her. She wasn't friends with anyone in the class and nobody ever tried to speak to her.

Marigold did not welcome attention in ballet class or at any other time. She was slightly plump and unfortunately also quite tall for her age. Her mother, who had been a moderately successful fashion model in her youth, was nearly 6 ft and it looked like Marigold was going to take after her mother in height. Sadly it looked as though she had inherited her father's stockier frame to go with it and the result was someone who would blend in better on a rugby pitch than bobbing around a dance studio in tights and a leotard: a llama amongst a herd of adorable little lambs.

All requests to drop ballet had been refused by her mother who had made up her mind that a girl as ungainly as Marigold needed to dance to develop some grace and poise. Marigold was fairly certain these were not qualities one could acquire....she was pretty sure you had to be born with them. But her mother would not listen to reason and for two long years she had put up with humiliation every Saturday.

And every week she annoyed her mother intensely by trying to get out of dance class. She'd make a hypochondriac proud with the number of headaches, colds, stomach aches, injuries from PE during the week at school, sleepless nights and many other fictitious ailments that struck her down at the last moment. All to no avail. Her mother would just purse her lips and tell her to 'suck it up, Marigold' or if she was in a better mood she'd tell her to 'put more effort in Marigold; you might enjoy it if you tried a bit harder.'

She could never win. Either she annoyed her mother or she irritated Miss Valentina and both were terrifying when roused but at least dance class only lasted for an hour. So in the end, every week she capitulated, pulled on the embarrassing leotard and got in the car.

This year had so far been slightly better since the arrival of Jarrod. Having a boy in the class meant there was someone else who was as conspicuous as her. Not that he seemed to care. He appeared oblivious to the spotlight that being the token male had inadvertently created.

After the Harry Potter comment, Marigold was almost looking forward to the next ballet class to see whether Jarrod would come out with something as amusing. Unfortunately, Miss Valentina had decided that the next Saturday's class would herald the start of rehearsals for the end of year recital. The prospect of the parents, by and large a doting bunch, who were convinced that their little darlings were dance protégés and were thus expecting to see a performance worthy of the Bolshoi, was too much pressure for Miss V. In the run up to the end of year recital her Russian outbursts became more frequent and she made it clear that she felt life was very unfair in having landed her with such a useless group of dunderheads to turn into dancers.

The painful process of learning a dance for the recital would commence with Miss Valentina teaching them all two or three steps, demonstrating the sequence with precision and delicacy. They would then be asked to try and imitate her moves, usually executing them with all the grace and elegance of donkeys in tights. Their efforts would upset Miss V so much that she would call them all to a halt by shrieking:

"Nyet, nyet, nyet……"

Then she'd demonstrate the sequence again and around and around the cycle they would go. Eventually she'd give up and move on to teach them the next steps and gradually, week after painful week, they put together their recital dance.

As this was Jarrod's first year at Miss Valentina's he had never experienced this process and his muttered comments in response to Miss V's flowery explosions flowed freely. Although this time Marigold had the sense to hide her responses, his witty remarks lifted Marigold's mood no end.

After class Marigold waited in the foyer for her mother to come and collect her. Jarrod strolled up and stood next to her. He looked at his phone and sighed:

"Late again….."

"Who?" asked Marigold.

"My Dad……" Jarrod pulled a face. "He does it on purpose….to make a point."

"What point?"

"That he disapproves of me doing ballet."

"Why does he disapprove of you doing ballet?"

Jarrod didn't answer. Instead he changed the subject:

"Do you like dancing?" He asked.

"I don't know…." Marigold felt dumb as soon as the words were out of her mouth. How could she not know whether she liked it or not? He stared at her and she knew she'd have to explain herself.

"It's not that I don't like ballet. I just don't like myself doing ballet. I'm a clumsy lump and I always disappoint Miss Valentina, no matter how hard I try."

"Oh, no, that's not true," said Jarrod, "you've got that wrong….."

Marigold was about to ask what he meant when a car horn suddenly tooted, the driver pressing the horn for an excessively long time, clearly signalling annoyance. Jarrod pulled a face.

"Gotta go; that's my Dad."

Marigold watched him walk to the car and as Jarrod pulled open the passenger door she saw the profile of a man, looking stony faced and grim at the wheel. He didn't turn to look at Jarrod as he got in but the second the door closed, the car sped away from the curb so fast, the tires squealed.

Marigold mulled over the conversation with Jarrod on and off for the whole of the next week. She was confused by what he'd said. Did he mean she wasn't bad at dancing? Was he implying that she wasn't a lump? But she was equally as curious about why he persisted in carrying on with dancing if his father was giving him such a hard time about it. She thought it pretty funny that she didn't want to dance and her mother made her go and Jarrod did want to dance but his father didn't want him to. Why was it you never got the parents you wanted?

Next week as the pupils all streamed in for class she deliberately sat down next to Jarrod to put on her ballet slippers. She asked him what he had meant about her dancing and Miss Valentina's constant criticism.

"Oh, Miss Valentina only makes a fuss about people getting it right if they're quite good at dancing. If she thinks you're a no hoper she's much more pleasant. When you're really bad she just 'very nice', well," Jarrod paused and grinned at Marigold, "actually she says: *vezzy niice.*" Marigold grinned back at him; Jarrod was too good at that accent but she still wasn't convinced he knew what he was talking about.

"Are you sure?"

Marigold had been in this class for a long time now and she'd rarely heard Miss Valentina praise anyone.

"Yup, I'm sure. Don't you remember Marie….from term one? Her dancing was always *vezzy niice* and she never came back after Easter."

Marigold thought back to the start of the year and a gangly girl who'd joined the class briefly. Marie was a shy girl and danced stiffly with wooden arms. Her long limbs seemed incapable of flexing in the way Miss Valentina required but she couldn't remember Miss Valentina ever exploding at Marie.

She didn't get any more time to talk with Jarrod as Miss Valentina barked at them all to get into position at the barre. After class her mother was waiting outside the building and she couldn't linger to chat but the following Saturday her mother was late again and she joined Jarrod in the foyer.

"Why do you keep going with dancing if your dad gives you a hard time about it?" Marigold asked him.

"I do it to annoy him."

"Why?"

Jarrod shrugged and stared hard at Marigold. He seemed about to say more when a gaggle of five girls, all blonde, slim and pretty, skipped past, chatting. They turned to stare at Marigold and Jarrod and one of them called out:

"Is Jarrod your boyfriend Marigold?"

Another girl added to their collective amusement with a barbed comment:

"Hope you don't step on his toes when you're kissing him his much as you stomp on mine in class, Marigold…..you're such a klutz!"

The group dissolved into fits of giggles. Marigold and Jarrod were silent for a moment and then Jarrod said:

"By and large, I don't like people much."

"Neither do I" said Marigold.

They stood together for a few minutes, not speaking, the silence growing awkward and heavy between them, digging a gulf that the last few weeks of tentative friendship might not have the strength to bridge. Marigold longed to say something witty or something clever, which would erase the embarrassment they were both feeling so acutely but she was lost for words. Marigold would be the first to admit that she was clumsy but as far as she could remember she had never actually trodden on that girl's toes….or anyone's toes in fact.

As for the boyfriend comment, she had no idea what Jarrod might be thinking. The idea that someone would link the two of them probably revolted him. She was trying not to feel hurt by the girls' comments but she was trying even harder not to feel hurt that the idea of being Jarrod's girlfriend might have horrified him so much he could no longer talk to her. They were saved by the arrival of Marigold's mother. She muttered a hasty "see ya," and bolted out of the door.

Marigold spent a miserable week, willing time to move more slowly and wishing she could come up with a fool proof escape from the next lesson. But Marigold was a pragmatic girl and knowing that she could not give up dance class for good, she also realised there was little point in prolonging an agony that was inevitable. She dragged herself most reluctantly into Miss Valentina's ballet school on Saturday morning.

To her surprise Jarrod sat next to her as she was putting on her shoes and flung his arm around her shoulders, planting a big kiss on her cheek.

"Hiya girlfriend," he trilled loudly enough for everyone in the room to hear, even over the noise of chattering girls and departing parents. Marigold's mouth dropped open. For a split second she wondered if Jarrod might be a bit crazy but he leaned in and whispered in her ear.

"Just go with it, I have a plan....." she stared at him and he nodded encouragingly.

"Hi Jarrod," she replied as cheerfully as she could, "I really enjoyed dinner at your place, it was great." He grinned at her and whispered again:

"Perfect.....talk to you after class."

Marigold's head was buzzing and she found it very hard to concentrate which was unfortunate. She drew attention from Miss V all morning who stopped the class three times to make Marigold repeat a particular bit of the dance when she kept muddling the sequence of steps.

"Marigold," Miss V sighed after the second time, "zis iz too much.....I don't know how many timz I 'av to say it: you are too stiff. You are not toy soldier in Nutcracker, you are butterfly. You float, you fly.....where iz ze flourish? I want more flourish!"

After class, Jarrod was waiting in the foyer for her.

"What's the deal, Jarrod?" Marigold asked, getting straight to the point.

"I decided we needed more flourish." Jarrod was grinning from ear to ear and Marigold was now certain he was crazy.

"What are you talking about?"

"I figured it out....it's just like the dancing and my dad," he said, sitting down and patting the floor next to him. She sat down and waited for something that made sense to come out of his mouth.

"You see, my Mum and Dad split up last year. Dad left us to move in with this new woman. Now he's got a new baby too. He wasn't interested in me at all for ages.....it was like I didn't exist. I mean, he pretended he cared....made a big fuss when he moved out that we'd see each other every other weekend but when I was at his place, it was like I was invisible."

"Oh Jarrod, I'm so sorry....."

"It's okay....."Jarrod paused and Marigold could tell that it wasn't okay but there was nothing she could think of to say that would make it better. Jarrod carried on.

"Then I decided to take up ballet. I wanted to do hip hop really but the only place that teaches it is all the way across town from us, so Mum suggested Miss V and ballet. I wasn't keen until it came up when I was at Dad's one night. He hit the roof. He got so mad and said I wasn't allowed to do it. I'd finally got his attention over something so I told Mum the next day that I was in. I dance because Dad can't ignore it. It bothers him so much and it makes him angry but now he notices me."

"Jarrod, I don't get what this has to do with those girls and what they said last week."

"Well, sometimes you need to do the opposite of what people tell you. They wanted to make you feel bad about being my girlfriend. So I figure if we pretend that we are going out together, what can they say? We win. They look stupid."

Marigold thought about it for a bit. She was pretty sure nobody else in the class had a boyfriend. They were kind of young for that sort of thing. So was Jarrod right? Would this change everything?

"Come on Marigold, what have you got to lose?"

"Okay," she said slowly, "I guess we could give it a try."

He grinned at her and put his arm around her shoulders and, as two stragglers walked past them on their way out of the dance studio, he pulled her towards him and kissed her loudly on the lips.

From that day, their friendship grew into a bond that gradually extended to life beyond ballet school. They never became a real couple but for the next year they pretended every Saturday. Their friendship, at first just solace for two young souls trying to navigate the challenges of adolescence, became the springboard that allowed them both to move confidently into adulthood.

Miss Valentina never managed to develop them into ballet stars but both Jarrod and Marigold would be the first to credit her and her ballet class with providing an opportunity to have lives lived with more flourish.

"His Father's Son", by Kerry Lown Whalen

On the outskirts of Stanton in rural Queensland, Blue ran sheep on the three thousand hectares his parents had left him. His flock-scattered paddocks nestled among fields of ripening corn, wheat and sorghum.

Most Saturdays he drank with his mates at the Royal where spilt pretzels, peanuts and crisps crunched underfoot and the stink of beer, sweat and fried onions stung his eyes. One afternoon, a girl walked in bringing the midday glare. She stood blinking, dress translucent in the light. For a moment she paused before strolling to a table in the corner.

As Blue slouched in his usual spot at the bar, his mate prodded him. 'Here's ya chance, bachelor boy.' Scotty leaned close. 'She's a looker and she's looking your way.'

Blue straightened up, lanky yet muscular in his checked shirt and jeans. Although women liked the look of him, they'd never stuck around for long. He ambled over. 'I'm Blue. What's your poison?'

Her eyes creased at the corners. 'White wine.'

'Got a name?'

'Val.'

He returned to the bar. 'Another schooner, Jim. And a white wine for Val.'

'Two white wines coming up,' the barman said.

His mates hooted when Blue gave him the finger. He walked back to her table and pulled out a chair. 'What's brought you to Stanton?'

'Just passing through.'

'That's what they all say.'

She leaned on her elbows. 'Is it worth staying?'

'Reckon it is. I'm here aren't I?' He winked.

She laughed.

The drinks kept coming and so did the laughs.

'I was a receptionist at a motel in Monto. Bor–ing. Today I walked out. Now I'm off to see my folks in Toowoomba.'

'Mon–to. Bor–ing. Too–woom–ba. Could be song lyrics.'

She had dimples when she smiled. 'I'll be driving home tomorrow.'

He nodded. 'Staying at the pub overnight?'

'Yep.'

He studied her. She was about twenty-five, with dark eyes and long wavy hair. After a few kids she'd be chubby, the way he liked his women.

'Why not stay at my place? It's just off the highway.'

She considered him through thick lashes. 'Can I trust you?'

He chuckled. 'Hey fellas. Val wants to know if she can trust me.'

His mates guffawed and Scotty shouted, 'He's an axe murderer. Don't turn your back.'

Val grinned. 'I won't.'

As the weeks turned into months the pair settled into a routine. While Blue looked after the property and sheep, Val fed the chooks, tended the vegetable garden and kept house. If Blue was in the mood they ate breakfast on the veranda. To the accompaniment of crow, cockatoo and currawong calls, they'd linger over cups of tea before starting their chores.

Val leaned back, steam unfurling from her cup. 'Sometimes you're talkative. Other times I can't get a word out of you. How come?'

'Dunno. Dad was the same.'

'Moody?'

'Very.'

'He take off into the mulga without a word like you do?'

'Yep.' He folded his arms.

'I worry when you're out there alone.'

'You shouldn't. I've always done it. I just need time to myself.'

'I get lonely.' She touched his hand.

He sighed. 'The bush calms me Val. Sometimes I've just got to get away.'

'Reckon that's why you're not married?'

'Probably. Plus I'm boring. Ignorant.'

'You could read newspapers and books. Watch TV. Then you'd be interesting.'

He pushed back his chair and reached for his boots. 'What you see is what you get.' He stood. 'I'll be in the back paddock. Fencing.'

By day's end every muscle in Blue's body ached. Even on a good day he didn't feel like talking, listening or thinking when eating his dinner. While Val tidied the kitchen he soaked in a hot bath, steam blurring the mirror and dripping down the walls. He climbed into bed at nine o'clock.

'D'you ever invite your mates over for a barbie?' Val asked, turning off the bed lamp.

'No.'

'Why not?'

'Too tired.'

'Their wives must be lonely. It's isolated out here.'

He turned onto his side. 'They've got chores to do. Kids to mind.'

'Let's invite Scotty and Jen over. I could do with some company.'

'Nuh.'

'What about me and what I want?'

'Give me a break Val.' He pulled the covers up around his ears.

For the rest of the week Blue didn't say much. While tucking into breakfast on Sunday he noticed Val pushing eggs and bacon around her plate.

'What's up?'

'Dad's sick. I've got to go home.'

Val's mother had rung the night before. 'When are you leaving?'

'This arvo.'

He reached for her hand. 'I'll miss you.'

'I should be back next weekend.'

When Val hadn't returned by Saturday Blue drove to town, stocked up on supplies and drifted into the Royal.

'Haven't seen you for ages.' Scotty punched his arm. 'Val keep you on a short leash?'

'Nuh.' Blue grinned. 'I'm not going to share Val with you.'

'So – why are you here?'

'She's in Toowoomba. Her dad's sick.'

Scotty's eyebrows shot up. 'Is that what she said?'

'Heard something different?'

He paused. 'I don't want to cause trouble.'

Blue frowned. 'What's the story?' His eyes held Scotty's as he drained his schooner.

'Jim saw Val in Toowoomba. She was acting all lovey-dovey with a fella from the council.'

Blue showed the barman his empty glass and turned to Scotty. 'Waddya mean, lovey-dovey?'

'Holding hands. Pashing.'

'Did Jim say that?'

'Yep. She waved to him.'

Jim plonked Blue's beer on the bar, froth spilling over the sides. 'It's true, mate. She didn't care who saw her.'

Blue tried to slow his breathing, his eyes fixed on the sluggish blades of a pedestal fan. Why would Val wave to Jim if she was with another bloke? It didn't make sense. Perhaps his mates were pulling his leg. He drummed his fingers. If he drove to Toowoomba he could sort it out. But it was a long drive and he was upset. In the end he finished his beer, went home and fed the dogs. After having a wash he rang Val and gave her an earful.

'Stop shouting,' she said. 'Everyone can hear you.' Her footsteps clattered on wooden boards. 'I'm on the porch. I can talk now.'

'Who's this bloke you've been seeing?'

She groaned. 'I saw Jim and waved, for heaven's sake. I wasn't hiding.'

The beer churned in his gut. 'Who is he?'

'My brother. Doug. He works at the council.'

'Yeah right! That's why you were pashing him.'

'I wasn't. Jim's having you on.'

Val hadn't talked much about her family, but had mentioned Doug. She hadn't said he worked at the council, but why would she? Perhaps his mates were taking the piss. They often did that. But surely they wouldn't make up stuff about Val.

'Have I got the wrong end of the stick?'

'Yep.'

He hesitated. 'How's your father?'

'You don't believe he's sick, do you?'

What was her problem? She'd been away for a week and he wanted her back. Was there something wrong with that? 'You've been away for ages.'

'Dad's having scans. X-rays.'

His stomach dived. It sounded serious. 'Want me to drive down? Scotty can look after things while I'm away. He can feed the dogs. The chooks.'

'No. I'm pissed-off. You believed Jim. Didn't ask me.'

'Sorry Val.'

'I don't feel like coming back now.'

'You've got to.' He hated begging but couldn't help himself. 'I miss you.'

She snorted. 'I'll see how I feel.' She didn't say goodbye.

Blue grabbed a stubbie from the fridge and mooched out to the veranda. He leaned on the rail and stared into the blackness, swigging from the bottle until it was empty. His eyes filled with tears. He told himself to grow up and lurched inside for another beer. Bile rose in his throat when he thought of the trouble Jim had caused. Shortly before midnight he grabbed the ute keys, drove to the pub and stood waiting at the back door. Already he wished he hadn't come. He should've gone to bed and had a good night's sleep like a normal person.

Shouts of farewell and doors slamming signalled closing time. Blue's chest pounded when Jim stepped outside and saw him in the shadows.

'What's up mate?'

'I'm not ya mate you bloody liar.'

Jim chuckled. 'Sucked in fella.'

One look at Jim's smirking face and Blue's fist shot into his cheekbone. Off-balance, Jim fell backwards and cracked his head on the step.

Blue shook his shoulder. 'Jim. Hey Jim!' A dark stain pooled on the step. 'Shit.' He felt Jim's chest. It thumped. Blue whipped out his mobile and called triple-zero.

'Send an ambulance to the pub quick. Jim's taken a tumble out the back. Hit his head on a step.'

He sprinted to the ute, fumbled with the ignition and roared into the night. He shouldn't have driven half-tanked to the pub or punched Jim. But it was too late for regrets now. He had to get out of town.

When the first rays of light gilded the hilltops, he crept into the national park. Although the cops might guess where he'd gone, there was no way they'd find him.

His breath came in ragged bursts as he slogged through the scrub, his legs screaming for rest after three days' hard march. Finally he flung down his swag and leaned back against an ironbark. The sun warmed his skin as he watched a stream of meat ants scurry past, clambering over twigs and leaves to their domed nest. Harmony reigned among the rough-barked gums, saplings and mulga. He wanted to stay, but had to keep moving. With a groan, he hefted his swag and trudged towards the gorge.

Grasping at whipstick and saltbush he slithered down to a pool of stagnant water. Torrential downpours often caused creeks to overflow, flushing out the river, but only scant rain had fallen in recent months. It meant setting off on a long hike upstream to find fresh water and food. He knew of a spot teeming with yabbies. Already he could taste them.

Magpies and cockatoos warned the dozing bush of his approach while crows alerted him to a stinking carcass beside the track. A mangled rabbit lay tangled in the spinifex, tempting bait for yabbies. He skewered the rotting mess with a stick and carried it like a rifle over his shoulder, a haze of flies squabbling around his head.

At the sound of water sloshing over stones he lengthened his stride, peering through spotted gums for the creek that fed the river. The track led there. He shrugged off his swag and lowered the carcass into the water. He pictured yabbies feasting on it as he collected kindling. When he hoisted the bait from the water, it crawled with crustaceans. He could've fed a family on what he caught.

He tossed his catch into the bubbling billy. The tinder crackled and spat, smoke spiralling skywards as he gorged on the sweet steaming flesh. He gathered up more sticks and litter, heaped them onto the embers and watched them blaze orange and red. It'd taken three days in the bush to clear his head. Now he could think straight.

By the time darkness and cold air swept along the creek he had decided to go home. If Val was there he'd do his best to sort things out. Afterwards he'd talk to the cops.

Blue slept soundly that night soothed by the soughing and sighing scrub. The sounds reminded him of childhood, of camping in the bush with his father. When he was nine he remembered his father standing in the doorway of his room.

'I need to talk. Man to man.'

Blue set aside his homework. 'What about?'

'Me. I'm going bush.'

'Why?'

'The black dog's got me.'

'What's the black dog?'

A tic flickered in his father's cheek. 'Dark moods. Sadness.'

'Let me come.'

His father shook his head. 'I'm lousy company. Can't talk.'

'We don't have to talk.'

He tousled Blue's hair, his face thoughtful. 'I'd like you to come.'

It was the first of many forays into the bush with his father. Blue had learned to shoot rabbits and 'roos, catch cod and yabbies, sleep rough and appreciate nature. He had matched his father's silence, focusing instead on the muttering mulga, cries of the wild and his beating heart. Without noticing, the bush had crept into his soul and quietened demons he hadn't known he possessed.

His world fell apart when his mother died from a heart attack. Then two days after his twentieth birthday he'd found his father's body hanging from a beam in the shearing shed. Blue didn't cry. He couldn't.

Left on his own Blue had devoted his time and energy to running the property. It was a lonely life. Before Val arrived, two live-in partners had come and gone. They'd had reason to go, had wanted more from him than he could give. Women liked to talk and socialise. He remembered the days when his mother had spread the white lace cloth over the dining room table and set it with silverware, gilt-edged crockery, platters of bite-sized sandwiches, pikelets, scones, cream and jam, its centrepiece a strawberry-and-cream sponge. Most of all, he remembered the chatter and laughter, the gaiety of his mother and her friends. He couldn't relate to their world – felt excluded from it. Women, and their talk, confused him.

He'd relaxed when Val had moved in, admiring the way she'd fitted into his routine, demanding little of him. Attractive and easygoing, she must have had previous relationships. He'd never asked. Nor had he shown interest in her family. And although he enjoyed having her around, he didn't tell her. Val was unaware of the difference she'd made to his life and of the depth of his feelings for her.

To avoid the cops, neighbours and sticky-beaks, Blue headed home after sunset. As he plodded along the dirt road to his property, dogs barked and strained on their chains. He snicked shut the front gate, boots crunching on gravel as he approached the house. His kelpies leapt about yelping. He ignored them. A light glowed from the brass lamp in the kitchen. Was Val home? His pulse raced.

He dropped his swag, slipped off his boots and padded across the veranda. The radio played. Through the window he saw Val silhouetted in gold. She turned when he opened the door, dark hair framing her face. It revealed nothing.

'I need a bath.' He moved towards her.

She kept the table between them. 'I tried to phone you.'

'I've been out of range. How's your dad?'

'Early stages of bowel cancer.'

He flinched. 'Will he be okay?'

'I think so.' She switched off the radio and approached him. 'We have to talk.'

He gripped her elbows, looked into her eyes. 'I've missed you.'

She pulled away, handed him a blue form. 'The cops left this.'

He'd seen a summons before but this was handwritten.

Jim's in hospital. Pay his medical bills and he might drop the assault charge. Call me.

Constable Les Dyer had signed it.

He folded it in half. 'I punched Jim.'

'Why?'

'I couldn't bear the thought of …' He looked down at his feet. '… you with another man.'

'Jealous?'

'Yep.' He reddened. 'You're special, Val.'

She shrugged. 'Pity Dad had to get sick for you to realise that.'

'Sorry.'

'You keep things to yourself.' She reached for his hand. 'You'll have to open up if you want our relationship to flourish.'

'I know. And I'm ready.' Sweat beaded his forehead. 'I'd like to start with the black dog. And what it does to me.'

"The Final Raid", by Caitlyn Whyte

Fire roars from within the hall, accompanied by the laughter of carefree men. The raiders have just returned from their latest attack, and celebrations are in order. Wine flows freely amongst the men, the spoils of their victims loosening tongues and emboldening words. The thick timber walls of the hall are warmed through with boasting as challenges fly through the air like friendly knives. Dusk is falling and the final rays of sun pave the town with burnt gold.

Hidden amongst the revelry and dappled light, a small, hunched figure is darting between the shadows, drawing ever closer to a long wooden building on the outskirts of the village. Situated far away from the hall that houses the celebrations, at first glance this building seems to be isolated from the rest of the village, carelessly pushed to the side. An easy assumption to make, yet sharper eyes will notice the strength of the structure, the shine to the wooden beams that hold the corners in place, the quiet confidence of the place. Strength, wealth and prestige radiate from the very grain of the wood, yet its simple elegance and the tranquil surroundings lend a sense of warmth and peace.

The figure that stalks the shadows around this home happens to be female. She is close to eighteen years of age and her small stature belies her ferocity. There is no outward sign which discriminates her from others, yet she holds a fierce determination to succeed where others have failed. The determination born of one horror filled night...

The villagers are awoken in the middle of the night by the acrid stench of burning. Men and women run outside, half-dazed by sleep but fast awakening. Orders are shouted and people collide as the villagers hurry to put the fire out. There is an added sense of urgency underlying these movements; the winter has only just passed, leaving the land hard and bare, and the villagers are struggling to survive on meagre stores. And then from nowhere, the raiders come. They slide out of the shadows from every direction, surrounding the village. There is no warning until it is too late, the soft tread of feet and the gentle clinking of weapons drowned by the roar of flames. The villagers are caught unprepared, and it is a massacre. Some reach for picthforks, wood axes, chairs, anything to defend themselves, but it is all for nothing. There is too much smoke, too much chaos and the stench of fear hangs heavy in the air, smothering everything. It is over quickly, too quickly, the whisper of steel through flesh lost in the crackling of wood being devoured by the greedy flames.

No one survives...

The girl is closer to the house now. Blood pounds a quick tempo in her head as she reaches up to look carefully in the window. There they are; one woman and two children. Three victims, and one retribution...

The smell of burning is strong in her nose as the girl awakes. Blearily, she looks around her, and realises she has fallen asleep in the forest again. Waiting for her traps to yield something had taken its toll, and the few moments she had taken to rest her eyes had stretched on and on. She curses violently and creatively under her breath, trying frantically to work out how late it is. While it was no secret that she hunted game in the woods, it was equally well known that her mother despised these night time activities. Despite the fact that most of the villagers were grateful for the extra food, her talents had to be hidden. The girl groans, trying to work the stiffness out of cramped muscles, and thinking about the world of pain she will be in when she gets home...

Retreating into the shadows, the girl sits on her haunches and waits. Before that night, in a time long ago, waiting was a burden, a chore that bred frustration and tension. Hunting had been the first step toward learning the act of waiting, but it was death that made her a master.

She takes a deep breath, focuses on one thing at a time. Breathe, relax, and wait. The familiar calm of the hunt slides over her, a steady calm that trickles through her, drowning the anxiety blooming in her heart. She sits and watches the last strands of daylight drain out of the night sky, and she remembers...

The smell of burning is stronger now, and something feels wrong. There is a different smell in the fire, a sinister undercurrent that raises the hairs on the back of her neck. The girl starts to jog, and then run towards her home. An owl screams at she passes, heeding her to hurry, but she needn't have. The sight of the fire stops her dead in her tracks. Stranded on the outskirts of the village, she sees only red before her, as the fire devours the last of her home, the only home she has ever known.

Abruptly the scene releases its grip on her and she stumbles forward, yelling for someone, anyone who isn't gone. She trips over bodies as she runs, crunching sickeningly over some and vaulting high over others. She wants to stop and look at all of them, to remember friends, family and rivals alike. She wants to see none of them, to be far away and safe in ignorance. She wants everything and nothing, pain and darkness, to be numb and to forget it all. To smother the fire and be cold again. But she can't. So instead she runs.

Bodies are thick on the ground, dogs and horses as well as humans, and it is a long time before the girl comes across her parents. There is red painted across their backs, a sick dark red that has her retching and choking. The girl has come to hate that colour, and all that it means. She falls to her knees beside them, and the futile screams of the survivor pierce the midnight air...

It is darker now, the thick black of night enveloping her as she finally begins preparing. She cuts her clothes with her hunting knife and rubs dirt into her skin. The precautions are almost unnecessary; her long trek has left her as dirtied and bloodied as she needs to be. She goes through them anyway, knowing she has not come this far to start taking chances. She nicks her cheek, and a gash appears across her arm. It brings a smile to her face to think that the knife that has skinned and bled countless animals is now doing the same to her. A hollow smile devoid of warmth and light; the only smile that is left to her now. The wounds are shallow, and the sharp pain is a welcome reminder of what it is to feel. She waits a little longer, watching the hated colour crawl across her skin, and then she hears it. The bell that signals midnight. It is time...

It takes a long time for the girl to move from her parents' side. The embers of her life smoulder around her as she has struggles to numb her pain, to replace it with something else; a purpose. Blinded by grief, in the midst of despair, she has found a way to make the pain go away. Standing, she makes her way out of the village, feet kicking up clouds of still hot ash as she walks, unable to stand the scene of carnage any longer. She leaves everything behind, even the precious little things the fire has left untouched. The weight of death on her shoulders was all the reminder she needed of this night.

The girl walks the rest of the night and well into the morning. She doesn't feel fatigue; she doesn't feel anything. She has a plan, and it propels her forward with inexorable force. As she walks, she thinks, of a midnight promise born from the sharp pain of loss, and how it will be fulfilled...

A knock on the door. She knows it is her hand knocking, but a strange sense of detachment has come over her, the numbness she craves enveloping her in its sweet embrace. A woman answers the door, looking bewildered and irritated by the interruption to her sleep. She takes one look at the torn and tattered girl standing in her doorway and her expression changes. The woman ushers the girl inside, her compassion outweighing anything else. Questions are asked but her waiting has not been in vain, and she is ready with a barrage of sorrowful lies. It is not hard to convince this woman that the slender young girl before her is not a threat. The girl has found that people want you to be what they expect, nothing more, and while her story is fabricated the sadness that seeps out from her is real.

A bowl of soup appears from a pot hanging over the fire banked high for the night, and the woman bustles off to find spare clothes. A tiny flicker of doubt springs up in her mind, fanned by the kindness of this stranger. For the first time since she has started on her journey, she questions if what she is doing is right. But she knows that a flicker can quickly become a flame, and fire is dangerous, so she crushes the doubt in her mind and douses the fire before it can catch. She is cold now, cold in her heart and her mind, and deep down in her soul…

With nothing but the clothes on her back and the pain in her heart, the girl is crossing the countryside. She works on a new farm every day in return for a meal and a place to rest for the night. Her skills are well appreciated by the country folk, but the thanks they give rings hollow in her mind. She is far more interested in the stories they have to tell. The stories that they tell her as she works for them and eats their food, their faces wrung ragged with grief and pain. Stories of raiders passing through, taking everything; food, weapons, women. Stories of men who foolishly try and stop them. Men who try and save sisters, wives, and daughters, and who are cut down for their efforts. Men who try and take on the world. She makes a list of these people in her mind, and their names echo in her head day and night...

The names return now, and they strengthen her resolve. She sees the faces of women who lost sons, fathers who buried their little girls, husbands who were married for a week when their wives were killed, and worse. When the woman returns, the girl sees her as nothing but what she is; the wife of the leader of the raiders, the man who destroyed her life, and the lives of so many others.

She knows she must act. The woman turns away and in a heartbeat the girl moves, stifling a scream with her hand, drawing the knife and striking, once, twice, three times. The woman falls hard, life spilling hot and red from the wounds in her back. The girl closes her eyes, swaying, holding fast to one idea, one night, one promise. Too late to stop now, she races down a long hall and through an arched doorway into the other room; the children's room. One child is sleeping tucked in a ball, hands wound tightly in her blankets, back hunched against the outside world. The other has sprawled across the bed, legs tangled in the covers, his pillow spilled onto the floor.

Hand shaking, she draws the knife back, but something stops her. She may have to end their lives, but she can give them a final gift. Mercy, of a sort. Lowering the knife, she takes the boy's pillow and ends their lives quietly, her whispered apology heavy in the still air.

Back in the first room, the girl starts to write. The names appear on the wall, their sickening ink staining the wood.

Jonathon, Andrew, Sarah...

The blood runs thick and fast as the girl continues, scribing the raider's travels on a map made of pain.

Anthony, Leah, Michael...

She finishes with the names of her parents, ending her writing with a gruesome flourish, the wall now almost covered in words glistening in the candlelight. The girl sits the body of the woman next to the wall of the dead, lighting a candle to place next to her. The flickering flame casts long shadows on the walls that dance and sway with an hypnotic rhythm. Tearing her gaze from the morbid dance, the girl retreats into the surrounding forest, settles herself on the hard ground, and waits.

Time passes but it is hard to tell how much; everything feels like nothing and waiting is an old friend. It is several hours before the raider returns to his home. There is a faint pink tinge on the horizon, the first hint of dawn struggling to break into a dark world. The man opens the door, and the sight that greets him stops him dead in his tracks.

The girl has learnt many things as she travelled. She has learnt how intoxicating pain can be, how it can bring escape and peace, if only for a time. That is something else she has learned, that the quest for peace is as endless as it is futile. She has learnt that justice is a game played by kings and lords which the common may not enter. She has even learned that despite how cruel and empty the world can seem, there is kindness to be found there too. But most of all she has learnt that however painful it is to die, it is nothing compared to the agony of living.

From her place in the forest, she hears it, as she knew she would. What she has been waiting for all this time has finally come, and for this small moment she allows herself to feel, to revel in the pleasure that is building in her.

The futile screams of the survivor pierce the morning air, and she smiles.

www.ingramcontent.com/pod-product-compliance
Lightning Source LLC
Chambersburg PA
CBHW051122260626
47170CB00005B/1616